W9-BTI-264

GLORY RIDERS

Center Point Large Print

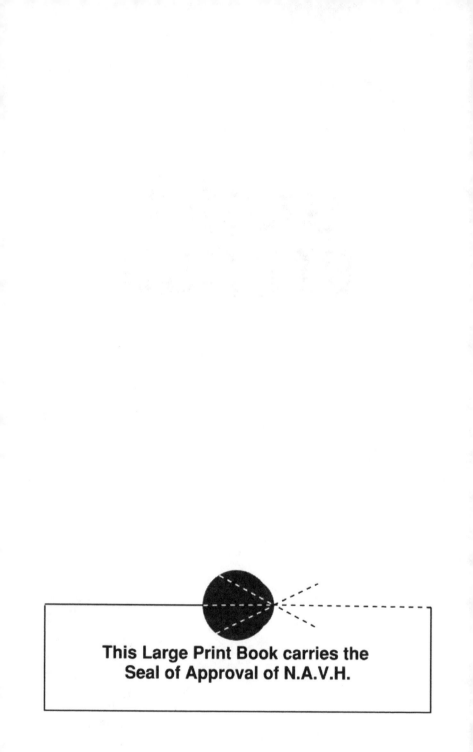

**This Large Print Book carries the
Seal of Approval of N.A.V.H.**

GLORY RIDERS

A Western Sextet

Louis L'Amour

Edited by
Jon Tuska

CENTER POINT PUBLISHING
THORNDIKE, MAINE

This Circle Ⓥ Western is published by
Center Point Large Print in 2011 in co-operation with
Golden West Literary Agency.

ISBN: 978-1-61173-107-1

Library of Congress Cataloging-in-Publication Data

L'Amour, Louis, 1908–1988.
Glory riders : a Western sextet / Louis L'Amour ; edited by Jon Tuska. — 1st ed.
p. cm.
ISBN 978-1-61173-107-1 (lib. bdg.)
1. Western stories. 2. Large type books. I. Tuska, Jon. II. Title.
PS3523.A446G56 2011
813′.52—dc22
                                                          2011007251

Acknowledgments

"Man Riding West" under the byline Jim Mayo first appeared in *West* (1/50). Copyright © 1949 by Better Publications, Inc. Copyright not renewed.

"The Turkeyfeather Riders" under the byline Jim Mayo first appeared in *West* (5/49). Copyright © 1949 by Better Publications, Inc. Copyright not renewed.

"Four Card Draw" under the byline Jim Mayo first appeared in *Giant Western* (2/51). Copyright © 1951 by Best Publications, Inc. Copyright not renewed.

"Home in the Valley" under the byline Jim Mayo first appeared in *Rio Kid Western* (8/49). Copyright © 1949 by Better Publications, Inc. Copyright not renewed.

"West is Where the Heart Is" by Louis L'Amour first appeared in *Popular Western* (4/51). Copyright © 1951 by Better Publications, Inc. Copyright not renewed.

"Fork Your Own Broncs" under the byline Jim Mayo first appeared in *Thrilling Ranch Stories* (5/47). Copyright © 1947 by Standard Magazines, Inc. Copyright not renewed.

Table of Contents

Foreword

by Jon Tuska

Louis Dearborn LaMoore (1908-1988) was born in Jamestown, North Dakota. He left home at fifteen and subsequently held a wide variety of jobs although he worked mostly as a merchant seaman. From his earliest youth, L'Amour had a love of verse. His first published work was a poem, "The Chap Worth While", appearing when he was eighteen years old in his former hometown's newspaper, the *Jamestown Sun*. It is the only poem from his early years that he left out of *Smoke From This Altar* which appeared in 1939 from Lusk Publishers in Oklahoma City, a book which L'Amour published himself; however, this poem is reproduced in *The Louis L'Amour Companion* (Andrews and McMeel, 1992) edited by Robert Weinberg. L'Amour wrote poems and articles for a number of small circulation arts magazines all through the early 1930s and, after hundreds of rejection slips, finally had his first story accepted, "Anything for a Pal" in *True Gang Life* (10/35). He returned in 1938 to live with his family where they had settled in Choctaw, Oklahoma, determined to make writing his career. He wrote a fight story bought by Standard Magazines that year and became acquainted with editor Leo Margulies who was to play an important rôle later in L'Amour's life. "The Town No Guns Could Tame" in *New Western* (3/40) was his first published Western story.

During the Second World War L'Amour was drafted and ultimately served with the U.S. Army Transportation Corps in Europe. However, in the two years before he was shipped out, he managed to write a great many adventure stories for Standard Magazines. The first story he published in 1946, the year of his discharge, was a Western, "Law of the Desert Born" in *Dime Western* (4/46). A talk with Leo Margulies resulted in L'Amour's agreeing to write Western stories for the various Western pulp magazines published by Standard Magazines, a third of which appeared under the byline Jim Mayo, the name of a character in L'Amour's earlier adventure fiction. The proposal for L'Amour to write new Hopalong Cassidy novels came from Margulies who wanted to launch *Hopalong Cassidy's Western Magazine* to take advantage of the popularity William Boyd's old films and new television series were enjoying with a new generation. Doubleday & Company agreed to publish the pulp novelettes in hard cover books. L'Amour was paid $500 a story, no royalties, and he was assigned the house name Tex Burns. L'Amour read Clarence E. Mulford's books about the Bar-20 and based his Hopalong Cassidy on Mulford's original creation. Only two issues of the magazine appeared before it ceased publication. Doubleday felt that the Hopalong character had to appear exactly as William Boyd did in the films and on television and thus the novels in book form had to be revamped to meet with this requirement prior to publication.

L'Amour's first Western novel under his own byline was *Westward the Tide* (World's Work, 1950). It was rejected by every American publisher to which it was submitted. World's Work paid a flat £75 without royalties for British Empire rights in perpetuity. L'Amour sold his first Western short story to a slick magazine a year later, "The Gift of Cochise" in *Collier's* (7/5/52). Robert Fellows and John Wayne purchased screen rights to this story from L'Amour for $4,000 and James Edward Grant, one of Wayne's favorite screenwriters, developed a script from it, changing L'Amour's Ches Lane to Hondo Lane. L'Amour retained the right to novelize Grant's screenplay, which differs substantially from his short story, and he was able to get an endorsement from Wayne to be used as a blurb, stating that *Hondo* was the finest Western Wayne had ever read. *Hondo* (Fawcett Gold Medal, 1953) by Louis L'Amour was released on the same day as the film, *Hondo* (Warner, 1953), with a first printing of 320,000 copies.

With *Showdown at Yellow Butte* (Ace, 1953) by Jim Mayo, L'Amour began a series of short Western novels for Don Wollheim that could be doubled with other short novels by other authors in Ace Publishing's paperback two-fers. Advances on these were $800 and usually the author never earned any royalties. *Heller with a Gun* (Fawcett Gold Medal, 1955) was the first of a series of original Westerns L'Amour had agreed to write under his own name following the success for Fawcett of *Hondo*. L'Amour wanted even this early to have his Western novels published in hard cover editions. He expanded "Guns of the Timberland" by Jim Mayo in *West* (9/50) for *Guns of the Timberlands* (Jason Press, 1955), a hard cover Western for which he was paid an advance of $250. Another novel for Jason Press followed and then *Silver Cañon* (Avalon Books, 1956) for Thomas Bouregy & Company.

The great turn in L'Amour's fortunes came about because of problems Saul David was having with his original paperback Westerns program at Bantam Books. Fred Glidden had been signed to a contract to produce two original paperback Luke Short Western novels a year for an advance of $15,000 each. It was a long-term contract but, in the first ten years of it, Fred only wrote six novels. Literary agent Marguerite Harper then persuaded Bantam that Fred's brother, Jon, could help fulfill the contract and Jon was signed for eight Peter Dawson Western novels. When Jon died suddenly before completing even one book for Bantam, Harper managed to engage a ghost writer at the Disney studios to write these eight "Peter Dawson" novels, beginning with *The Savages* (Bantam, 1959). They proved inferior to anything Jon had ever written and what sales they had seemed to be due only to the Peter Dawson name.

Saul David wanted to know from L'Amour if *he* could deliver two Western novels a year. L'Amour said he could, and he did. In fact, by 1962 this number was increased to three original paperback novels a year. The first L'Amour novel to appear under the Bantam contract was *Radigan* (Bantam, 1958).

Yet I feel that some of Louis L'Amour's finest work is to be found in his early magazine fiction. Several of those stories are collected here, reprinted as they first appeared, and possessing the characteristics in purest form that I suspect account in largest measure for the loyal following Louis L'Amour won from his readers: the young male hero who is in the process of growing into manhood and who is evaluating other human beings and his own experiences; a resourceful frontier woman who has beauty as well as fortitude; and the powerful, romantic, strangely compelling vision of the American

West that invests L'Amour's Western fiction and makes it such a delightful escape from the cares of a later time—in this author's words, that "big country needing big men and women to live in it" and where there was no place for "the frightened or the mean."

GLORY RIDERS

A Western Sextet

MAN RIDING WEST

Three men were hunkered down by the fire when Jim Gary walked his buckskin up to their camp in the lee of the cliff. The big man across the fire had a shotgun lying beside him. It was the shotgun that made Gary uneasy, for cowhands do not carry shotguns, especially when on a trail drive, as these men obviously were.

Early as it was, the cattle were already bedded down for the night in the meadow alongside the stream, and from their looks they had come far and fast. It was still light, but the clouds were low and swollen with rain.

"How's for some coffee?" Jim asked as he drew up. "I'm riding through, and I'm sure hungry and tuckered."

Somewhere off in the mountains, thunder rolled and grumbled. The fire crackled, and the leaves on the willows hung still in the lifeless air. There were three saddled horses nearby, and among the gear was an old Mother Hubbard-styled saddle with a wide skirt.

"Light an' set up." The man who spoke was lean-jawed and sandy-haired. "Never liked to ride on an empty stomach myself."

17

More than ever, Gary felt uneasy. Neither of the others spoke. All were tough-looking men, unshaven and dirty, but it was their hard-eyed suspicion that made Jim wonder. However, he swung down and loosened his saddle girth, and then slipped off the saddle and laid it well back under the overhang of the cliff. As he did so, he glanced again at the old saddle that lay there.

The overhang of the cliff was deep where the fire was built for shelter from the impending rain. Jim dropped to an ancient log, gray and stripped of bark, and handed his tin plate over to the man who reached for it. The cook slapped two thick slabs of beef on the plate and some frying-pan bread liberally touched with the beef shavings. Gary was hungry and he dived in without comment, and the small man filled his cup.

"Headed west?" the sandy-haired man asked, after a few minutes.

"Yeah, headed down below the rim. Pleasant Valley way."

The men all turned their heads toward him but none spoke. Jim could feel their eyes on his tied-down guns. There was a sheep and cattle war in the valley.

"They call me Red Slagle. These *hombres* are Tobe Langer and Jeeter Dirksen. We're drivin' to Salt Creek."

Langer would be the big one. "My name's

Gary," Jim replied. "Jim Gary. I'm from points yonder. Mostly Dodge and Santa Fe."

"Hear they are hiring warriors in Pleasant Valley."

"Reckon." Jim refused to be drawn, although he had the feeling they had warmed to him since he mentioned heading for the valley.

"Ridin' thataway ourselves," Red suggested. "Want to make a few dollars drivin' cattle? We're short-handed."

"Might," Gary admitted. "The grub's good."

"Give you forty to drive to Salt Creek. We'll need help. From hereabouts the country is plumb rough, an' she's fixin' to storm."

"You've hired a hand. When do I start?"

"Catch a couple of hours' sleep. Tobe has the first ride. Then you take over. If you need help, just you call out."

Gary shook out his blankets and crawled into them. In the moment before his eyes closed, he remembered the cattle had all worn a Double A brand, and the brands were fresh. That could easily be with a trail herd. But the Double A had been the spread that Mart Ray had mentioned.

It was raining when he rode out to the herd. "They ain't fussin'," Langer advised, "an' the rain's quiet enough. It should pass mighty easy. See you."

He drifted toward the camp, and Gary turned

up his slicker collar and studied the herd as well as he could in the darkness. They were lying quietly. He was riding a gray, roped from the small remuda, and he let the horse amble placidly toward the far side of the meadow. A hundred yards beyond the meadow the bulk of the sloping hill that formed the opposite side of the valley showed blacker in the gloom. Occasionally there was a flash of heat lightening, but no thunder.

Slagle had taken him on because he needed hands, but none of them accepted him. He decided to sit tight in his saddle and see what developed. It could be plenty, for, unless he was mistaken, this was a stolen herd, and Slagle was a thief, as were the others. If this herd had come far and fast, he had come farther and faster, and with just as great a need. Now there was nothing behind him but trouble, and nothing before him but bleak years of drifting ahead of a reputation.

Up ahead was Mart Ray, and Ray was as much a friend as he had. Gunfighters are admired by many, respected by some, feared by all, and welcomed by none. His father had warned him of what to expect, warned him long ago before he himself had died in a gun battle. "You're right handy, Son," he had warned, "one of the fastest I ever seen, so don't let it be known. Don't ever draw a gun on a man in anger, and you'll live happy. Once you get the name of a gunfighter, you're on a lonesome trail, and there's only one ending."

So he had listened, and he had avoided trouble. Mart Ray knew that. Ray was himself a gunman. He had killed six men of whom Jim Gary knew, and no doubt there had been others. He and Mart had been riding together in Texas and then on a couple of trail drives, one all the way to Montana. He never really got close to Mart, but they had been partners after a fashion.

Ray had always been amused at his eagerness to avoid trouble, although he had no idea of the cause of it. "Well," he had said, "they sure cain't say like father, like son. From all I hear your pappy was an uncurried wolf, an' you fight shy of trouble. You run from it. If I didn't know you so well, I'd say you was yaller."

But Mart Ray had known him well, for it had been Jim who rode his horse down in front of a stampede to pick Ray off the ground, saving his life. They got free, but no more, and a thousand head of cattle stampeded over the ground where Ray had stood.

Then, a month before, down in the Big Bend country, trouble had come, and it was trouble he could not avoid. It braced him in a little Mexican *cantina* just over the river, and in the person of a dark, cat-like Mexican with small feet and dainty hands, but his guns were big enough and there was an unleashed devil in his eyes.

Jim Gary had been dancing with a Mexican girl, and the Mexican had jerked her from his arms and struck her across the face. Jim knocked him down, and the Mexican got up, his eyes fiendish. Without a word, the Mexican went for his gun, and for a frozen, awful instant Jim saw his future facing him, and then his own hand went down and he palmed his gun in a flashing, lightning draw that rapped out two shots. The Mexican, who had reached first, barely got his gun clear before he was dead. He died on his feet, and then fell.

In a haze of powder smoke and anguish, Jim Gary had wheeled and strode from the door, and behind him lay a dead and awful silence. It was not until two days later that he knew who and what he had killed. The lithe-bodied Mexican had been Miguel Sonoma, and he had been a legend along the border. A tough, dangerous man with a reputation as a killer.

Two nights later, a band of outlaws from over the border rode down upon Gary's little spread to avenge their former leader, and two of them died in the first blast of gunfire, a matter of handguns at pointblank range. From the shelter of his cabin, Gary had fought them off for three days before the smoke from his burning barn attracted help. When the help had arrived, Jim Gary was a man with a name. Five dead men lay on the ground around the ranch yard and in the desert nearby. The wounded had been carried away. And the following morning, Jim turned his ranch over to the bank to sell and lit a shuck—away from Texas.

Of this, Mart Ray knew nothing. Half of Texas and all of New Mexico, or most of it, would lie behind him when Jim reached the banks of Salt Creek. Mart Ray was ramrodding the Double A, and he would have a job for him.

Jim Gary turned the horse and rode slowly back along the side of the herd. The cattle had taken their midnight stretch and, after standing around a bit, were lying down once more. The rain was falling, but softly, and Gary let the gray take his own time in skirting the herd.

The night was pitch dark. Only the horns of the cattle glistened with rain, and their bodies were darker blobs in the blackness of the night. Once, drawing up near the willows along the stream, Jim thought he detected a vague sound. He waited a moment, listening. On such a night nobody would be abroad who could help it, and it was unlikely that a mountain lion would be on the prowl, although possible.

He started on again, yet now his senses were alert, and his hand slid under his slicker and touched the butt of a .44. He was almost at the far end of the small herd when a sudden flash of lightning revealed the hillside across the narrow valley.

Stark and clear, glistening with rain, sat a horseman. He was standing in his stirrups, and seemed amazingly tall, and in the glare of the flash his face was stark white, like the face of a fleshless skull.

Startled, Gary grunted and slid his gun into his hand, but all was darkness again, and, listen as he could, he heard no further sound. When the lightning flashed again, the hillside was empty and still. Uneasily he caught himself staring back over his shoulder into the darkness, and he watched his horse. The gray was standing, head up and ears erect, staring off toward the darkness near the hill. Riding warily, Gary started in that direction, but when he got there, he found nothing.

It was almost daylight when he rode up to the fire that had been kept up throughout the night, and, swinging down, he awakened Dirksen. The man sat up, startled. "Hey!" he exclaimed. "You forget to call me?"

Jim grinned at him. "Just figured I was already up and a good cook needed his sleep."

Jeeter stared at him. "You mean you rode for me? Say, you're all right!"

"Forget it." Gary stretched. "I had a quiet night, mostly."

Red Slagle was sitting up, awakened by their talk. "What do you mean . . . mostly?"

Jim hesitated, feeling puzzled. "Why, to tell

you the truth, I'm not sure whether I saw anything or not, but I sure thought I did. Anyway, it had me scared."

"What was it?" Slagle was pulling on his pants, but his eyes were serious. "A lion?"

"No, it was a man on a horse. A tall man with a dead-white face, like a skull." Gary shrugged sheepishly. "Makes me sound like a fool, but I figured for a moment that I'd seen a ghost."

Red Slagle was staring at him, and Jeeter's face was dead-white and his eyes were bulging. "A ghost?" he asked faintly. "Did you say a ghost?"

"Shucks"—Gary shrugged—"there ain't no such thing. Just some *hombre* on a big black horse, passing through in the night, that was all. But believe me, seeing him in the lightning up on that hill like I did, it sure was scary."

Tobe Langer was getting up, and he, too, looked bothered. Slagle came over to the fire and sat down, boots in hand. Reaching down, he pulled his sock around to get a hole away from his big toe, then he put his foot into the wet boot, and began to struggle with it.

"That horse, now," Langer asked carefully, "did it have a white star between the eyes?"

Gary was surprised. "Why, yes. Matter of fact, it did. You know him?"

Slagle let go of the boot and stomped his foot to settle it in the boot. "Yeah, feller we seen down the road a ways. Big black horse."

Slagle and Langer walked away from camp a ways, and stood talking together. Jeeter was worried. Jim could see that without half trying, and he studied the man thoughtfully. Jeeter Dirksen was a small man, quiet, but inclined to be nervous. He had neither the strength nor the toughness of Slagle and Langer. If Gary learned anything about the cattle, it would be through his own investigation or from Jeeter. And he was growing more and more curious.

Yet if these were Double A cattle and had been stolen, why were they being driven toward the Double A Ranch, rather than away from it? He realized suddenly that he knew nothing at all about Red Slagle or his outfit, and it was time he made some inquiries.

"This Double A," he asked suddenly, "you been riding for them long?"

Dirksen glanced at him sharply and bent over his fire. "Not long," he said. "It's a Salt Creek outfit. Slagle's *segundo*."

"Believe I know your foreman," Gary suggested. "I think this was the outfit he said. *Hombre* name of Mart Ray. Ever hear of him?"

Jeeter turned sharply, slopping coffee over the rim of the cup. It hissed in the fire, and both the other men looked around at the camp. Jeeter handed the cup to Gary and studied him, searching his face. Then he admitted cautiously: "Yeah, Ray's the foreman. Ranch belongs to a syndicate out on the coast. You say you know him?"

"Uhn-huh. Used to ride with him." Langer and Slagle had walked back to the fire, and Dirksen poured coffee for them.

"Who was that you rode with?" Slagle asked.

"Your boss, Mart Ray."

Both men looked up sharply, then Slagle's face cleared and he smiled. "Say, that's why the name was familiar. You're *that* Jim Gary. Son of old Steve Gary. Yeah, Mart told us about you."

Langer chuckled suddenly. "You're the scary one, huh? The one who likes to keep out of trouble. Yeah, we heard about you."

The contempt in his tone stiffened Jim's back, and for an instant he was on the verge of a harsh retort. Then the memory of what lay behind him welled up within, and bitterly he kept his mouth shut. If he got on the prod and killed a man here, he would only have to drift farther. There was only one solution, and that was to avoid trouble. Yet, irritating as it was to be considered lacking in courage, Langer's remark let him know that the story of his fights had not preceded him.

"There's no call," he said after a minute, "to go around the country killing folks. If people would just get the idea they can get along without all that. Me, I don't believe in fighting."

Langer chuckled, but Slagle said nothing, and Dirksen glanced at him sympathetically.

27

• • •

All day the herd moved steadily west, but now Gary noticed a change, for the others were growing more watchful as the day progressed. Their eyes continued to search the surrounding hills, and they rode more warily approaching any bit of cover.

Once, when Jeeter rode near him, the little man glanced across the herd at the other riders and then said quietly: "That was no ghost you saw. Red rode up there on the hill, an' there was tracks, tracks of a mighty big black horse."

"Wonder why he didn't ride down to camp?" Jim speculated. "He sure enough saw the fire."

Dirksen grunted. "If that *hombre* was the one Red thinks it is, he sure didn't have no aim to ride down there."

Before Gary could question him further, Jeeter rode off after a stray and, cutting him back into the herd, rode on farther ahead. Jim dropped back to the drag, puzzling over this new angle. Who could the strange rider be? What did he want? Was he afraid of Slagle?

A big brindle steer was cutting wide of the herd, and Jim swung out to get him, but, dashing toward the stream, the steer floundered into the water and into quicksand. Almost at once, it was down, struggling madly, its eyes rolling.

Jim swung a loop and dropped it over the steer's horns. If he could give the steer a little

28

help now, there was a chance he could get it out before it bogged in too deep.

He started the buckskin back toward more solid ground and with the pull on the rope and the struggling of the steer, he soon had it out on the bank of the stream. The weary animal stumbled and went down, and, shaking his loop loose, Gary swung his horse around to get the animal up. Something he saw on the flank made him swing down beside the steer. Curiously he bent over the brand.

It had been worked over. The Double A had been burned on over a Slash Four.

"Something wrong?"

The voice was cold and level, and Jim Gary started guiltily, turning. Then his eyes widened. "Mart! Well, for crying out in the nighttime. Am I glad to see you."

Ray stared. "For the luvva Pete, if it ain't Gary! Say, how did you get here? Don't tell me you're driving that herd up ahead?"

"That's right. Your outfit, ain't it? I hired on back down the line. This steer just got himself bogged down and I had a heck of a time getting him out. You seen Red and the boys?"

"Not yet. I swung wide. Get that steer on his feet and we'll join 'em."

Yet, as they rode back, despite Ray's affability, Gary was disturbed. Something here was very wrong. This was a Slash Four steer with the brand worked over to a Double A, the brand for which Ray was foreman. If these cattle were rustled, then Mart Ray was party to it, and so were Slagle, Langer, and Dirksen. And if he was caught with these men and cattle, so was he.

He replied to Ray's questions as well as he could, and briefly, aware that his friend was preoccupied and thinking of something else. Yet at the same time he was pleased that Ray asked him no questions about his reasons for leaving home.

Mart Ray rode up ahead and joined Slagle, and he could see the two men riding on together, deep in conversation. When they bedded down for the night, there had been no further chance to talk to him, and Gary was just as well satisfied, for there was much about this that he did not like. Nor was anything said about the midnight rider. When day broke, Mart Ray was gone. "Rode on to Salt Creek," Red said. "We'll see him there." He glanced at Jim, his eyes amused. "He said to keep you on, that you was a top hand."

Despite the compliment, Jim was nettled. What else had Ray told Slagle? His eyes narrowed. Whatever it was, he was not staying on. He was going to get shut of this outfit just as fast as he could. All he wanted was his time. Yet by midday he had not brought himself to ask for it.

Dirksen had grown increasingly silent, and he avoided Langer and Slagle. Watching him, Jim was puzzled by the man, but could find no reason for his behavior unless the man was frightened by something. Finally Jim pulled up alongside Jeeter.

The man glanced at him and shook his head. "I don't like this. Not even a little. She's too quiet."

Gary hesitated, waiting for the cowhand to continue, but he held his peace. Then, Gary said, speaking slowly: "It is mighty quiet, but I see nothing wrong with that. I'm not hunting trouble."

"Trouble," Jeeter said dryly, "comes sometimes whether you hunt it or not. If anything breaks around this herd, take my advice an' don't ask no questions. Just scatter dust out of here."

"Why are you warning me?" Gary asked.

Jeeter shrugged. "You seem like a right nice feller," he said quietly. "Shame for you to get rung in on somethin' as dirty as this when you had nothin' to do with it."

Despite his questions, Jeeter would say no more, and finally Gary dropped back to the drag. There was little dust because of the rains, but the drag was a rough deal, for the herd was tired and the cattle kept lagging back. Langer and Slagle, Jim observed, spent more time watching the hills than the cattle. Obviously both men were as jumpy as Dirksen and were expecting something. Toward dusk Red left the herd and rode up a cañon into the hills.

Slagle was still gone, and Jim was squatting by the fire watching Jeeter throw grub together when there was a sudden shot from the hills to the north.

Langer stopped his nervous pacing and faced the direction of the shot, his hand on his gun. Jim Gary got slowly to his feet, and he saw that Jeeter's knuckles gripping the frying pan were white and hard.

Langer was first to relax. "Red must have got him a turkey," he said. "Few around here, and he was sayin' earlier he'd sure like some."

Nevertheless, Gary noted that Langer kept back from the firelight and had his rifle near at hand. There was a sound of an approaching horse, and Langer slid his rifle across his knees, but it was Slagle. He swung down, glancing toward the big man. "Shot at a turkey an' missed." Then he added, looking right at Langer: "Nothin' to worry about now. This time for sure."

Dirksen got suddenly to his feet. "I'm quittin', Red. I don't like this a-tall, not none. I'm gettin' out."

Slagle's eyes were flat and ugly. "Sit down an' shut up, Jeeter," he said impatiently. "Tomorrow's our last day. We'll have a payday this side of Salt Creek, an' then, if you want to blow, why you can blow out of here."

Gary looked up. "I reckon you can have my

time then, too," he said quietly. "I'm riding west for Pleasant Valley."

"You?" Langer snorted. "Pleasant Valley? You better stay somewhere where you can be took care of. They don't side-step trouble out there."

Gary felt something rise within him, but he controlled his anger with an effort. "I didn't ask you for any comment, Tobe," he said quietly. "I can take care of myself."

Langer sneered. "Why, you yaller skunk. I heard all about you. Just because your pappy was a fast man, you must think folks are skeered of you. You're yaller as saffron. You ain't duckin' trouble. You're just scared."

Gary was on his feet, his face white. "All you've got to do, Tobe, if you want to lose some teeth, is to stand up."

"What?" Langer leaped to his feet. "Why, you dirty. . . ."

Jim Gary threw a roundhouse left. The punch was wide, but it came fast, and Langer was not expecting Jim to fight. Too late he tried to duck, but the fist caught him on the nose, smashing it and showering the front of his shirt with gore.

The big man was tough, and he sprang in, swinging with both hands. Gary stood his ground, and began to fire punches with both fists. For a full minute the two big men stood toe to toe and slugged wickedly, and then Gary deliberately gave ground. Overeager, Langer leaped after him, and Gary brought up a wicked right that stood Tobe on his boot toes, and then a looping left that knocked him into the fire.

With a cry, he leaped from the flames, his shirt smoking. Ruthlessly Gary grabbed him by the shirt front and jerked him into a right hand to the stomach and then a right to the head, and shoving him away he split his ear with another looping left, smashing it like an overripe tomato. Langer went down in a heap.

Red Slagle had made no move to interfere, but his eyes were hard and curious as he stared up at Gary. "Now where," he said, "did Ray get the idea that you wouldn't fight?"

Gary spilled water from a canteen over his bloody knuckles. "Maybe he just figured wrong. Some folks don't like trouble. That doesn't mean they won't fight when they have to."

Langer pulled himself drunkenly to his feet and staggered toward the creek.

Red measured Jim with careful eyes. "What would you do," he asked suddenly, "if Langer reached for a gun?"

Gary turned his level green eyes toward Slagle. "Why, I reckon I'd have to kill him," he said matter-of-factly. "I hope he ain't so foolish."

Dawn broke cold and gray, and Jim Gary walked his horse up into the hills where he heard the shot the night before. He knew that, if Slagle saw him, he would be in trouble, but there was much he wanted to know.

Despite the light fall of rain the night before, there were still tracks. He followed those of Slagle's bay until he found where they joined those of a larger horse. Walking the buckskin warily, Jim followed the trail. It came to a sudden end.

A horse was sprawled in the clearing, shot through the head. A dozen feet away lay an old man, a tall old man, his sightless eyes staring toward the lowering skies, his arms flung wide. Jim bent over him and saw that he had been shot three times through the chest. Three times. And the wound lower down was an older wound, several days old, at least.

The horse wore a Slash Four brand. Things were beginning to make sense now. Going through the old man's pockets, Jim found a worn envelope containing some tallies of cattle, and the envelope was addressed to *Tom Blaze, Durango, Colo.*

Tom Blaze . . . the Slash Four. Tom Blaze, the pioneer Kiowa-fighting cattleman who owned the Slash Four, one of the toughest outfits in the West. Why he had not connected the two, Jim could not imagine, but the fact remained that the Slash Four had struck no responsive chord in his thoughts until now. And Tom Blaze was dead.

Now it all fitted. The old Mother Hubbard

saddle had been taken from Tom's horse, for this was the second time he had been shot. Earlier, perhaps when the cattle had been stolen, they had shot him and left him for dead, yet they had been unable to leave the saddle behind, for a saddle was two or three months' work for a cowhand and not to be lightly left behind.

They had been sure of themselves, too. Sure until Gary had seen Blaze, following them despite his wound. After that they had been worried, and Slagle must have sighted Blaze the afternoon before and then followed him and shot him down.

When the Slash Four found Tom Blaze dead, all hell would break loose. Dirksen knew that, and that was why he wanted out, but fast. And it was why Red Slagle and Tobe Langer had pushed so hard to get the cattle to Salt Creek, where they could be lost in larger herds or in the breaks of the hills around the Double A.

When he rode the buckskin down to the fire, the others were all up and moving around. Langer's face was swollen and there were two deep cuts, one on his cheek bone, the other over an eye. He was sullen and refused to look toward Gary.

Slagle stared at the buckskin suspiciously, noticing the wetness on his legs from riding in the high grass and brush.

Whatever the *segundo* had in mind he never

got a chance to say. Jim Gary poured a cup of coffee, but held it in his left hand. "Red, I want my money. I'm taking out."

"Mind if I ask why?" Red's eyes were level and waiting.

Gary knew that Slagle was a gun hand, but the thought did not disturb him. While he avoided trouble, it was never in him to be afraid, nor did his own skill permit it. While he had matched gun speed with only one man, he had that sure confidence that comes from unerring marksmanship and speed developed from long practice.

"No, I don't mind. This morning I found Tom Blaze's body, right where you killed him yesterday afternoon. I know that Slash Four outfit, and I don't want to be any part of this bunch when they catch up to you."

His frankness left Slagle uncertain. He had been prepared for evasion. This was not only sincerity, but it left Slagle unsure as to Gary's actual stand. From his words Slagle assumed Gary was leaving from dislike of fight rather than dislike of rustling.

"You stick with us, Jim," he said. "You're a good man, like Mart said. That Slash Four outfit won't get wise, and there'll be a nice split on this cattle deal."

"I want no part of it," Jim replied shortly. "I'm out. Let me have my money."

"I ain't got it," Red said simply. "Ray pays us all off. I carry no money around. Come on, Jim, lend us a hand. We've only today, then we'll be at the head of Salt Creek Wash and get paid off."

Gary hesitated. He did need the money, for he was broke and would need grub before he could go on west. Since he had come this far, another day would scarcely matter. "All right, I'll finish the drive."

Nothing more was said, and within the hour they moved out. Yet Gary was restless and worried. He could feel the tenseness in the others and knew they, too, were disturbed. There was no sign of Mart Ray, who should be meeting them soon.

To make matters worse, the cattle were growing restive. The short drives had given them time to recover some of their energy, and several of them, led by one big red steer, kept breaking for the brush. It was hot, miserable work. The clouds still hung low, threatening rain, but the air was sultry.

Jim Gary started the day with the lean gray horse he had ridden before, but by mid-afternoon he had exchanged the worn-out animal for his own buckskin. Sweat streamed down his body under his shirt, and he worked hard, harrying the irritable animals down the trail that now was lined with piñon and juniper, with a sprinkling of huge boulders. Ahead, a wide cañon opened, and not far beyond would be the spot where he expected to find Ray with the pay-off money.

The big red steer suddenly made another bolt for the brush, and the buckskin unwound so fast that it almost unseated Gary. He swore softly and let the horse take him after the steer and cut it back to the herd. As it swung back, he glanced up to see Langer and Red Slagle vanishing into the brush. Where Dirksen was he could not guess until he heard a wild yell.

Swinging around, he saw a dozen hard-riding horsemen cutting down from the brush on both sides, and a glance told him that flight was useless. Nevertheless, Jeeter Dirksen tried it.

Slamming the spurs into his bronco, Dirksen lunged for the brush in the direction taken by Slagle and Langer, but he had made no more than a dozen yards when a rattle of gunfire smashed him from the saddle. His slender body hit the ground rolling, flopped over one last time, and lay, sprawled and sightless, under the low gray clouds.

Gary rested his hands on his saddle horn and stared gloomily at the strange little man, so badly miscast in this outlaw venture. Then horsemen closed in around him; his six-guns were jerked from their holsters and his rifle from its scabbard.

"What's the matter with you?" The voice was harsh. "Won't that horse of yours run?"

Jim looked up into a pair of cold gray eyes in a leather-like face. A neat gray mustache showed above a firm-lipped mouth. Jim Gary smiled, although he had never felt less like it in his life. The horsemen surrounded him, and their guns were ready. "Never was much of a hand to run," Jim said, "and I've done nothing to run for."

"You call murderin' my brother nothin'? You call stealin' cattle nothin'? Sorry, friend, we don't see things alike. I call it hangin'."

"So would I, only I haven't done those things. I hired onto this outfit back down the line. Forty bucks to the head of Salt Creek Wash . . . and they ain't paid me."

"You'll get paid!" The speaker was a lean, hard-faced young man. "With a rope!"

Another rider, a girl, pushed a horse through the circle. "Who is this man, Uncle Dan? Why didn't he try to get away?"

"Says he's just a hired hand," Uncle Dan commented.

"That's probably what that dead man would have said, too!" the lean cowpuncher said. "Let me an' the boys have him under that cottonwood we seen. It had nice strong limbs."

Gary had turned his head to look at the girl. Uncle Dan would be Dan Blaze, and this must be the daughter of the murdered man. She was tall and slim, but rounded of limb and undeniably attractive, with color in her cheeks and a few scattered freckles over her nose. Her eyes were hazel and now looked hard and stormy.

"Did you folks find Tom Blaze's body?" he asked. "They left him back yonder." Lifting a hand carefully to his shirt pocket, he drew out the envelope and tally sheets. "These were his."

"What more do you need?" the lean cowpuncher demanded. He pushed his horse against Jim's and grabbed at the buckskin's bridle. "Come on, boys!"

"Take it easy, Jerry!" Dan Blaze said sharply. "When I want him hung, I'll say so." His eyes shifted back to Jim. "You're a mighty cool customer," he said. "If your story's straight, what are you doing with these?"

As briefly as possible, Jim explained the whole situation and ended by saying: "What could I do? I still had forty bucks coming, and I did my work, so I aim to collect. You say there were three men with the herd? And the two who got away were Tobe Langer and Red Slagle?"

"That's right," Jim hesitated over Mart Ray, and then said no more.

Blaze was staring at the herd, and now he looked at Jim. "Why were these cattle branded Double A? That's a straight outfit. You know anything about that?"

Gary hesitated. Much as he had reason to believe Ray was not only one of these men but

41

their leader, he hated to betray him. "Not much. I don't know any of these outfits. I'm a Texas man."

Blaze smiled wryly. "You sound it. What's your handle?"

"Jim Gary."

The cowpuncher named Jerry started as if struck. "Jim Gary?" he gasped, his voice incredulous. "The one who killed Sonoma?"

"Yeah, I reckon."

Now they were all staring at him with new interest, for the two fights he had were ample to start his name growing a legend on the plains and desert. These cowpunchers had heard of him, probably from some grubline rider or drifting cowpuncher.

"Jim Gary," Blaze mused. "We've heard about you. Old Steve's son, aren't you? I knew Steve."

Jim looked up, his eyes cold. "My father," he said grimly, "was a mighty good man."

Dan Blaze's eyes warmed a little. "You're right. He was."

"What of it?" Jerry demanded sullenly. "The man's a killer. We know that. We found him with the cattle. We found him with some of Tom's stuff on him. What more do you want?"

The girl spoke suddenly. "There was another rider, one who joined you and then rode away. Who was he?"

There it was, and Jim suddenly knew he would

not lie. "Mart Ray," he said quietly, "of the Double A."

"That's a lie!" The girl flashed back. "What are you saying?"

"You got any proof of that?" Jerry demanded hotly. "You're talkin' about a friend of our'n."

"He was a friend of mine, too." Gary explained about Mart Ray. "Why don't you turn me loose?" he suggested then. "I'll go get Ray and bring him to you. Chances are Slagle and Tobe will be with him."

"You'll get him?" Jerry snorted. "That's a good one, that is."

"Tie him," Dan Blaze said suddenly. "We'll go into Salt Creek."

Riding behind Dan Blaze and his niece, who he heard them call Kitty, Jim Gary was suddenly aware, almost for the first time, of the danger he was in. The fact that it had been averted for the moment was small consolation, for these were hard, desperate men, and one of their number, perhaps more, had been slain.

Fear was something strange to him, and, while he had known danger, it had passed over him, leaving him almost untouched. This situation conveyed only a sense of unreality, and until now the idea that he might really be in danger scarcely seemed credible. Listening to these men, his mind changed about that. He realized belatedly that he was in the greatest danger of his life. If he had none of their talk to warn him, the mute evidence of Jeeter's body was enough. And Jeeter had died yelling to him, trying to give him a warning so he might escape.

Now fear rode with him, a cold, clammy fear that stiffened his fingers and left his mouth dry and his stomach empty. Even the sight of the scattered buildings of the town of Salt Creek did not help, and, when they rode up the street, the red of embarrassment crept up his neck at the shame of being led into the town, his hands tied behind him, like a cheap rustler.

Mart Ray was sitting on the steps, and he shoved his hat back and got to his feet. Beside him was Red Slagle. There was no sign of Tobe Langer. "Howdy, Dan! What did you catch? A hoss thief?" Ray's voice was genial, his eyes bland. "Looks like a big party for such a small catch."

Blaze reined in his horse and stopped the little cavalcade. His eyes went from Mart to Slagle. "How long you been here, Red?" he demanded.

"Me?" Slagle was innocent. "No more'n about fifteen minutes, maybe twenty. Just rode in from the Double A. Somethin' wrong?"

Blaze turned his cold eyes on Jim Gary, and then looked back to Ray. "We found a herd of Slash Four cattle east of here, Mart. They were wearin' a Double A brand worked over our Slash Four. How do you explain it?"

Ray shrugged. "I don't," he said simply. "How does that *hombre* you got with you explain it?"

Kitty Blaze spoke up quickly: "Mart, did you ever see this man before? Did you?"

Ray stared at Gary. "Not that I recall," he said seriously. "He sure don't look familiar to me."

"Blaze," Gary said suddenly, "if you'll turn my hands loose and give me a gun, I can settle this in three minutes. I can prove he's a liar. I can prove that he does know me and that I know him."

"There's nothin' you can prove with a gun you can't prove without it," Blaze said flatly. "Whatever you know, spill it. Else you're gettin' your neck stretched. I'm tired of this fussin' around."

Jim Gary kneed his horse forward. His eyes were hot and angry. "Mart," he said, "I always suspected there was a streak of coyote in you, but I never knew you'd be this low-down. I don't like to remind anybody of what I did for him, but I recall a stampede I hauled you out of. Are you going to talk?"

Ray shook his head, smiling. "This is a lot of trouble, Dan. Take him away and stretch his neck before I get sore and plug him."

"You'd be afraid to meet me with a gun, Mart. You always were afraid," Jim taunted. "That's why you left Red and Tobe with the cattle. You wanted the profit but none of the trouble. Well, you've got trouble now. If I had a gun, I'd see you eat dirt."

Mart Ray's face was ugly. "Shut up, you fool! You call me yellow? Why, everybody knows you're yellow as . . . !" He caught himself abruptly, his face paling under the tan.

"What was that, Ray?" Dan Blaze's face had sharpened. "Everybody knows what about him? If you've never seen him before, how could you say everybody calls him yellow?"

Ray shrugged. "Just talkin' too fast, that's all!" He turned and stepped up on the sidewalk. "He's your man. You settle your own war." Ray turned to go, but Jim yelled at him, and Ray wheeled.

"Mart, if I don't know you, how do I know you've got a white scar down your right side, a scar made by a steer's hoof?"

Ray laughed, but it was a strained laugh. He looked trapped now, and he took an involuntary step backward. "That's silly," he scoffed. "I've no such scar."

"Why not take off your shirt?" Jerry said suddenly. "That will only take a minute." The lean-jawed cowhand's face was suddenly hard. "I think I remember you having such a scar, from one time I seen you swimmin' in the San Juan. Take off your shirt an' let's see!"

Mart Ray backed up another step, his face sharp and cold. "I'll be damned if I take off my

46

shirt in the street for any low-down rustler," he snapped. "This here nonsense has gone far enough."

"Loose my hands," Jim pleaded in a whisper. "I'll take his shirt off."

Kitty stared at him. Her face was white and strained, but in her eyes he now saw a shadow of doubt. Yet it was Jerry who acted suddenly, jerking him around before anyone realized what he had done and severing the bonds with a razor-sharp knife and jerking the ropes from his hands. With almost the same gesture, he slammed guns in Gary's holsters. "All right. Maybe I'm crazy," he snapped. "But go to it."

The whole action had taken less than a minute, and Mart Ray had turned his back and started away while Blaze waited in indecision. It was Red Slagle who saw Jim Gary hit the ground. "Boss!" he yelled. His voice was suddenly sharp with panic. "Look out!"

Ray wheeled, and, when he saw Gary coming toward him, chafing his wrists, he stood still, momentarily dumbfounded. Then he laughed. "All right, yellow. You're askin' for it. This is one bunch of trouble you can't duck. You've ducked your last fight."

Furious, he failed to realize the import of his words, and he dropped into a half crouch, his hands ready above his gun butts. It was Jerry who shook him, Jerry who made the casual remark that jerked Mart Ray to realization of what he was facing.

"Looks like whatever Ray knows about him, he sure ain't heard about Jim Gary killin' Miguel Sonoma."

Mart Ray was staggered. "Sonoma?" he gasped. "You killed Sonoma?"

Jim Gary was facing him now. Some of the numbness was gone from his hands, and something cold and terrible was welling up within him. He had ridden beside this man, shared food with him, worked with him, and now the man had tricked and betrayed him. "Yes, Mart, I killed Sonoma. I ain't afraid. I never was. I just don't like trouble."

Ray's tongue touched his lips and his eyes narrowed to slits. He sank a little deeper into the crouch, and men drew away to the sides of the street. Scarcely twenty feet apart, the two faced each other. "Take off your shirt, Ray. Take if off and show them. Reach up slow and unbutton it. You take it off yourself, or I'll take it off your body."

"Go to blazes!" Ray's voice was hoarse and strange. Then, with incredible swiftness, his hands dropped for his guns.

In the hot, dusty stillness of the afternoon street, all was deathly still. Somewhere a baby cried, and a foot shifted on the boardwalk. For what seemed an age, all movement seemed frozen and still as the two men in the street faced each other.

Kitty Blaze, her eyes wide with horror, seemed caught in that same breathless time-frozen hush. The hands of the men were moving with flashing speed, but at that instant everything seemed to move hauntingly slow. She saw Mart Ray's gun swing up; she saw the killing eagerness in his face, his lips thinned and white, his eyes blazing. And she saw the stranger, Jim Gary, tall, lithe, and strong, his dark face passionless, yet somehow ruthless. And she saw his lean brown hand flash in a blur of movement, saw flame leap from the black muzzles of his guns, and saw Mart Ray smashed back, back, back! She saw his body flung sideways into the hitching rail, saw a horse rear, his lashing hoofs within inches of the man. She saw the gun blaze again from the ground, and a leap of dust from the stranger's shoulder, and she saw Gary move coolly aside to bring his guns better to bear upon the man who was now struggling up. As in a kind of daze, she saw Jim Gary holding his fire, letting Ray get to his feet. In that stark, incredible instant, she saw him move his lips and she heard the words, as they all heard them in the silence of the street. "I'm sorry, Mart. You shouldn't have played it this way. I'd rather it had been the stampede."

And when Ray's guns swung up, his shirt was bloody, his face twisted in a sort of leer torn into his cheek by a bullet, and his eyes were fiendish. The guns came up, and even as they came level, red flame stabbed from the muzzles of Gary's guns and Ray's body jerked, dust sprang from his shirt's back, and he staggered back and sat down on the edge of the walk, and then, as though taken with a severe pain in the groin, he rolled over into the street and sprawled out flat. Somewhere thunder rolled.

For a long moment, the street was motionless. Then somebody said: "We better get inside. She's rainin'."

Jerry swung from his horse and in a couple of strides was beside the fallen man. Ripping back the shirt, he exposed the side, scarred by a steer's hoof.

Dan Blaze jerked around. "Slagle!" he yelled. "Where's Red Slagle! Get him!"

"Here." Slagle was sitting against the building, gripping a bloody hand. "I caught a slug. I got behind Ray." He looked up at Blaze. "Gary's right. He's straight as a string. It was Ray's idea to ring him in and use him as the goat after he found him with us."

Dan Blaze knelt beside him. "Who killed my brother?" he demanded. "Was it you or Ray?"

"Ray shot him first. I finished it. I went huntin' him an' he busted out of the brush. He had a stick he'd carried for walkin' an' I mistook it for a gun."

"What about Langer?" Gary demanded. "Where is he?"

Red grinned, a hard, cold grin. "He lit a shuck. That whuppin' you gave him took somethin' out of him. Once he started to run, he didn't stop, not even for his money." He dug into his pocket. "That reminds me. Here's the forty bucks you earned." Jim Gary took the money, surprised speechless. Slagle struggled erect. Gary's expression seemed to irritate him. "Well, you earned it, didn't you? An' I hired you, didn't I? Well, I never gypped no man out of honest wages yet. Anyway," he added wryly, "by the looks of that rope I don't reckon I'll need it. Luck to you, kid." He grinned. "Stay out of trouble."

Thunder rumbled again, and rain poured into the street, a driving, pounding rain that would start the washes running and bring the grass to life again, green and waving for the grazing cattle, moving west, moving north.

THE TURKEYFEATHER RIDERS

Jim Sandifer swung down from his buckskin and stood for a long minute, staring across the saddle toward the dark bulk of Bearwallow Mountain. His was the grave, careful look of a man accustomed to his own company under the sun and in the face of the wind. For three years he had been riding for the B Bar, and for two of those years he had been ranch foreman. What he was about to do would bring an end to that, an end to the job, to the life here, to his chance to win the girl he loved.

Voices sounded inside the ranch house, the low rumble of Gray Bowen's bass and the quick, light voice of his daughter Elaine. The sound of her voice sent a quick spasm of pain across Sandifer's face. Tying the buckskin to the hitch rail, he ducked under it and walked up the steps, his boots sounding loudly on the planed boards, his spurs tinkling lightly.

The sound of his steps brought instant stillness to the group inside and then the quick tattoo of Elaine's feet as she hurried to meet him. It was a sound he would never tire of hearing, a sound that had brought gladness to him such as he had never known before. Yet when her eyes met his at the door, her flashing smile faded.

"Jim! What's wrong?" Then she noticed the blood on his shoulder and the tear where the bullet had ripped his shirt, and her face went white to the lips. "You're hurt!"

"No . . . only a scratch." He put aside her detaining hand. "Wait. I'll talk to your dad first." His hands dropped to hers, and, as she looked up, startled at his touch, he said gravely and sincerely: "No matter what happens now, I want you to know that I've loved you since the day we met. I've thought of little else, believe that." He dropped her hands then and stepped past her into the huge room where Gray Bowen waited, his big body relaxed in a homemade chair of cowhide.

Rose Martin was there, too, and her tall, handsome son Lee. Jim's eyes avoided them for he knew what their faces were like; he knew the quiet serenity of Rose Martin's face, masking a cunning as cold and calculating as her son's flaming temper. It was these two who were destroying the B Bar, they who had brought the big ranch to the verge of a deadly range war by their conniving, a war that could have begun this morning, but for him.

Even as he began to speak, he knew his words

would put him right where they wanted him, that when he had finished, he would be through here, and Gray Bowen and his daughter would be left unguarded to the machinations of this woman and her son. Yet he could no longer refrain from speaking. The lives of men depended on it.

Bowen's lips thinned when he saw the blood. "You've seen Katrishen? Had a run-in with him?"

"No." Sandifer's eyes blazed. "There's no harm in Katrishen if he's left alone. No trouble unless we make it. I ask you to recall, Gray, that for two years we've lived at peace with the Katrishens. We have had no trouble until the last three months." He paused, hoping the idea would soak in that trouble had begun with the coming of the Martins. "He won't give us any trouble if we leave him alone."

"Leave him alone to steal our range!" Lee Martin flared.

Sandifer's eyes swung. "Our range? Are you now a partner in the B Bar?"

Lee smiled, covering his slip. "Naturally, as I am a friend of Mister Bowen's, I think of his interests as mine."

Bowen waved an impatient hand. "That's no matter. What happened?"

Here it was, then. The end of all his dreaming, his planning, his hoping. "It wasn't Katrishen. It was Klee Mont."

"Who?" Bowen came out of his chair with a lunge, veins swelling. "Mont shot you? What for? Why, in heaven's name?"

"Mont was over there with the Mello boys and Art Dunn. He had gone over to run the Katrishens off their Iron Creek holdings. If they had tried that, they would have started a first-class range war with no holds barred. I stopped them."

Rose Martin flopped her knitting in her lap and glanced up at him, smiling smugly. Lee began to roll a smoke, one eyebrow lifted. This was what they had wanted, for he alone had blocked them here. The others the Martins could influence, but not Jim Sandifer.

Bowen's eyes glittered with his anger. He was a choleric man, given to sudden bursts of fury, a man who hated being thwarted and who was impatient of all restraint. "You stopped them? Did they tell you whose orders took them over there? Did they?"

"They did. I told them to hold off until I could talk with you, but Mont refused to listen. He said his orders had been given him and he would follow them to the letter."

"He did right!" Bowen's voice boomed in the big room. "Exactly right! And you stopped them? You countermanded my orders?"

"I did." Sandifer laid it flatly on the line. "I told them there would be no burning or killing while I was foreman. I told them they weren't going to run us into a range war for nothing."

Gray Bowen balled his big hands into fists. "You've got a gall, Jim. You know better than to countermand an order of mine. And you'll leave me to decide what range I need. Katrishen's got no business on Iron Creek, an' I told him so. Told him to get off an' get out. As for this range war talk, that's foolishness. He won't fight."

"Putting them off would be a very simple matter," Lee Martin interposed quietly. "If you hadn't interfered, Sandifer, they would be off now and the whole matter settled."

"Settled nothing!" Jim exploded. "Where did you get this idea that Bill Katrishen could be pushed around? The man was an officer in the Army during the war, and he's fought Indians on the plains."

"You must be a great friend of his," Rose Martin said gently. "You know so much about him."

The suggestion was there, and Gray Bowen got it. He stopped in his pacing, and his face was like a rock. "You been talkin' with Katrishen? You sidin' that outfit?"

"This is my outfit. I ride for the brand," Sandifer replied. "I know Katrishen, of course. I've talked to him."

"And to his daughter?" Lee suggested, his eyes bright with malice. "With his pretty daughter?"

57

Out of the tail of his eye Jim saw Elaine's head come up quickly, but he ignored Lee's comment. "Stop and think," he said to Bowen. "When did this trouble start? When Missus Martin and her son came here. You got along fine with Katrishen until then. They've been putting you up to this."

Bowen's eyes narrowed. "That will be enough of that!" he said sharply. He was really furious now, not the flaring, hot fury that Jim knew so well, but a cold, hard anger that nothing could touch. For the first time Jim realized how futile any argument was going to be. Rose Martin and her son had insinuated themselves too much and too well into the picture of Gray Bowen's life.

"You wanted my report," Sandifer said quietly. "Mont wouldn't listen to my arguments for time. He said he had his orders and would take none from me. I told him then that if he rode forward it was against my gun. He laughed at me, then reached for his gun. I shot him."

Gray Bowen's widened eyes expressed his amazement. "You shot Mont? You beat him to the draw?"

"That's right. I didn't want to kill him, but I shot the gun out of his hand and held my gun on him for a minute to let him know what it meant to be close to death. Then I started them back here."

Bowen's anger was momentarily swallowed by his astonishment. He recalled suddenly that in

58

the three years Sandifer had worked for him there had been no occasion for him to draw a gun in anger. There had been a few brushes with Apaches and one with rustlers, but all rifle work. Klee Mont was a killer with seven known killings on his record and had been reputed to be the fastest gun hand west of the Río Grande.

"It seems peculiar," Mrs. Martin said composedly, "for you to turn your gun on men who ride for Mister Bowen, taking sides against him. No doubt you meant well, but it does seem strange."

"Not if you know the Katrishens," Jim replied grimly. "Bill was assured he could settle on that Iron Creek holding before he moved in. He was told that we made no claim on anything beyond Willow and Gilita Creeks."

"Who," Lee insinuated, "assured him of that?"

"I did," Jim said coolly. "Since I've been foreman, we've never run any cattle beyond that boundary. Iron Mesa is a block that cuts us off from the country south of there, and the range to the east is much better and is open for us clear to Beaver Creek and south to the Middle Fork."

"So you decide what range will be used? I think for a hired hand you take a good deal of authority. Personally I'm wondering how much your loyalty is divided. Or if it is divided. It seems to me you act more as a friend of the Katrishens . . . or their daughter."

Sandifer took a step forward. "Martin," he said evenly, "are you aiming to say that I'd double-cross the boss? If you are, you're a liar."

Bowen looked up, a chill light in his eyes that Sandifer had never seen there before. "That will be all, Jim. You better go."

Sandifer turned on his heel and strode outside.

When Sandifer walked into the bunkhouse, the men were already back. The room was silent, but he was aware of the hatred in the cold, blue eyes of Mont as he lay sprawled in his bunk. His right hand and wrist were bandaged. The Mello boys snored in their bunks, while Art Dunn idly shuffled cards at the table. These were the new hands, hired since the coming of the Martins. Only three of the older hands were in, and none of them spoke.

"Hello . . . lucky." Mont rolled up on his elbow. "Lose your job?"

"Not yet," Jim said shortly, aware that his remark brought a fleeting anger to Mont's eyes.

"You will," Mont assured him. "If you are in the country when this hand gets well, I'll kill you."

Jim Sandifer laughed shortly. He was aware that the older hands were listening, although none would have guessed it without knowing them.

"You called me lucky, Klee. It was you who

were lucky in that I didn't figure on killing you. That was no miss. I aimed for your gun hand. Furthermore, don't try pulling a gun on me again. You're too slow."

"Slow?" Mont's face flamed. He reared up in his bunk. "Slow? Why, you two-handed bluffer!"

Sandifer shrugged. "Look at your hand," he said calmly. "If you don't know what happened, I do. That bullet didn't cut your thumb off. It doesn't go up your hand or arm. The wound runs across your hand."

They all knew what he meant. Sandifer's bullet must have hit his hand as he was in the act of drawing and before the gun came level, indicating that Sandifer had beaten Mont to the draw by a safe margin. That Klee Mont realized the implication was plain, for his face darkened and then paled around the lips. There was pure hatred in his eyes when he looked up at Sandifer.

"I'll kill you," he said viciously. "I'll kill you."

As Sandifer started outside, Rep Dean followed him. With Grimes and Sparkman, he was one of the older hands.

"What's come over this place, Jim? Six months ago there wasn't a better spread in the country." Sandifer did not reply, and Dean built a smoke. "It's that woman," he said. "She twists the boss around her little finger. If it wasn't for you, I'd quit, but I'm thinkin' that there's nothin' she wouldn't like better than for all of the old hands to ask for their time."

Sparkman and Grimes had followed them from the bunkhouse. Sparkman was a lean-bodied Texan with some reputation as an Indian fighter.

"You watch your step," Grimes warned. "Next time Mont will back-shoot you!"

They talked among themselves, and, as they conversed, Sandifer ran his thoughts over the developments of the past few months. He had heard enough of Mrs. Martin's sly, insinuating remarks to understand how she had worked Bowen up to ordering Katrishen driven off, yet there was no apparent motive. It seemed obvious that the woman had her mind set on marrying Gray Bowen, but for that it was not essential that any move be made against the Katrishens.

Sandifer's limitation of the B Bar range had been planned for the best interests of the ranch. The range they now had in use was bounded by streams and mountain ranges and was rich in grass and water, a range easily controlled with a small number of hands and with little danger of loss from raiding Indians, rustlers, or varmints. His willingness to have the Katrishens move in on Iron Creek was not without the B Bar in mind. He well knew that range lying so much out of the orbit of the ranch could not be long held tenantless, and the Katrishens were stable, honest people who would make good neighbors and good allies. Thinking back, he could remember almost to the day when the first rumors began to spread, and most of them had stemmed from Lee Martin himself. Later, one of the Mello boys had come in with a bullet hole in the crown of his hat and a tale of being fired on from Iron Mesa.

"What I can't figure out," Grimes said, "is what that no-account Lee Martin would be doin' over on the Turkeyfeather."

Sandifer turned his head. "On the Turkeyfeather? That's beyond Iron Mesa. Why, that's clear over the other side of Katrishen's."

"Sure enough. I was huntin' that brindle steer who's always leadin' stock off into the cañons when I seen Martin fordin' the Willow. He was ridin' plumb careful, an' he sure wasn't playin' no tenderfoot then. I was right wary of him, so I took in behind an' trailed him over to that rough country near Turkeyfeather Pass. Then I lost him."

The door slammed up at the house, and they saw Lee Martin come down the steps and start toward them. It was dusk, but still light enough to distinguish faces. Martin walked up to Sandifer.

"Here's your time." He held out an envelope. "You're through."

"I'll want that from Bowen himself," Sandifer replied stiffly.

"He doesn't want to see you. He sent this note." Martin handed over a sheet of the coarse brown paper on which Bowen kept his accounts. On it, in Bowen's hand, was his dismissal.

I won't have a man who won't obey orders. Leave tonight.

Sandifer stared at the note, which he could barely read in the dim light. He had worked hard for the B Bar, and this was his answer.

"All right," he said briefly. "Tell him I'm leaving. It won't take any great time to saddle up."

Martin laughed. "That won't take time, either. You'll walk out. No horse leaves this ranch."

Jim turned back, his face white. "You keep out of this, Martin. That buckskin is my own horse. You get back in your hole and stay there."

Martin stepped closer. "Why, you cheap bigmouth!"

The blow had been waiting for a long time, but it came fast now. It was a smashing left that caught Martin on the chin and spilled him on his back in the dust. With a muttered curse, Martin came off the ground and rushed, but Sandifer stepped in, blocking a right and whipping his own right into Lee's mid-section. Martin doubled over, and Jim straightened him with a left uppercut, and then knocked him crashing into the corral fence.

Abruptly Sandifer turned and threw the saddle on the buckskin.

"Dammit, I'm quittin', too!" Sparkman said.

"An' me!" Grimes snapped. "I'll be dog-goned if I'll work here now."

Heavily Martin got to his feet. His white shirt was bloody, and they could vaguely see a blotch of blood over the lower part of his face. He limped away, muttering.

"Sparky," Jim said, low-voiced, "don't quit. All of you stay on. I reckon this fight ain't over, an' the boss may need a friend. You stick here. I'll not be far off."

Sandifer had no plan, yet it was Lee Martin's ride to the Turkeyfeather that puzzled him most, and almost of its own volition his horse took that route. As he rode, he turned the problem over and over in his mind, seeking for a solution, yet none appeared that was satisfactory. Revenge for some old grudge against the Katrishens was considered and put aside; he could not but feel that whatever the reason for the plotting of the Martins, there had to be profit in it somewhere.

Certainly there seemed little to prevent Rose Martin from marrying Gray Bowen if she wished. The old man was well aware that Elaine was a lovely, desirable girl. The cowhands and other male visitors who came to call for one excuse or another were evidence of that. She would not be with him long, and, if she left, he was faced with the dismal prospect of ending his years alone. Rose Martin was a shrewd woman and attractive for her years, and she knew how to make Gray comfortable and how to appeal to him. Yet, obviously, there was something more in her mind than this, and it was that something more in which Sandifer was interested.

Riding due east, Jim crossed Iron Mesa and turned west by south through the broken country. It was very late, and vague moonlight filtered through the yellow pine and fir that guarded the way he rode with their tall columns. Twice he halted briefly, feeling a strange uneasiness, yet listen as he might, he could detect no alien sound, nothing but the faint stirring of the slight breeze through the needles of the pines and the occasional rustle of a blown leaf. He rode on, but now he avoided the bright moonlight and kept more to the deep shadows under the trees.

After skirting the end of the Jerky Mountains, he headed for Turkeyfeather Pass. Somewhere off to his left, lost against the blackness of the ridge shadow, a faint sound came to him. He drew up, listening. He did not hear it again, yet his senses could not have lied. It was the sound of a dead branch scraping along leather, such a sound as might be made by a horseman riding through brush.

Sliding his Winchester from its scabbard, he rode forward, every sense alert. His attention was drawn to the buckskin, whose ears were up and who, when he stopped, lifted his head and stared off toward the darkness. Sandifer started the horse forward, moving easily.

To the left towered the ridge of Turkeyfeather Pass, lifting all of five hundred feet above him, black, towering, ominous in the moonlight. The trees fell away, massing their legions to right and left, but leaving before him an open glade, grassy and still. Off to the right Iron Creek hustled over the stones, whispering wordless messages to the rocks on either bank. Somewhere a quail called mournfully into the night, and the hoofs of the buckskin made light whispering sounds as they moved through the grass at the edge of the glade.

Jim drew up under the trees near the creek and swung down, warning the buckskin to be still. Taking his rifle, he circled the glade under the trees, moving like a prowling wolf. Whoever was over there was stalking him, watching a chance to kill him or perhaps only following to see where he went. In any case, Jim meant to know who and why.

Suddenly he heard a vague sound before him, a creak of saddle leather. Freezing in place, he listened and heard it again, followed by the crunch of gravel. Then he caught the glint of moonlight on a rifle barrel and moved forward, shifting position to get the unseen man silhouetted against the sky. Sandifer swung his rifle.

"All right," he said calmly, "drop that rifle and lift your hands. I've got you dead to rights."

As he spoke, the man was moving forward, and instantly the fellow dived headlong. Sandifer's rifle spat fire, and he heard a grunt, followed by a stab of flame. A bullet whipped past his ear. Shifting ground on cat feet, Jim studied the spot carefully.

The man lay in absolute darkness, but listening he could hear the heavy breathing that proved his shot had gone true. He waited, listening for movement, but there was none. After a while the breathing grew less and he took a chance.

"Better give up!" he said. "No use dying there!"

There was silence and then a slight movement of gravel. Then a six-shooter flew through the air to land in the open space between them.

"What about that rifle?" Sandifer demanded cautiously.

"Lost . . . for God's sake, help . . . me!"

There was no mistaking the choking sound. Jim Sandifer got up and, holding his rifle on the spot where the voice had sounded, crossed into the shadows. As it was, he almost stumbled over the wounded man before he saw him. It was Dan Mello, and the heavy slug had gone into his body but seemed not to have emerged.

Working swiftly, Jim got the wounded man into an easier position and carefully pulled his shirt away from the wound. There was no mistaking the fact that Dan Mello was hit hard. Jim gave the wounded man a drink, and then hastily built a fire to work by. His guess that the bullet had not emerged proved true, but, moving his hand gently down the wounded man's back, he could feel something hard near his spine. When he straightened, Mello's eyes sought his face.

"Don't you move," Sandifer warned. "It's right near your spine. I've got to get a doctor."

He was worried, knowing little of such wounds. The man might be bleeding internally.

"No, don't leave me," Mello pleaded. "Some varmint might come." The effort of speaking left him panting.

Jim Sandifer swore softly, uncertain as to his proper course. He had little hope that Mello could be saved, even if he rode for a doctor. The nearest one was miles away, and movement of the wounded man would be very dangerous. Nor was Mello's fear without cause, for there were mountain lions, wolves, and coyotes in the area, and the scent of blood was sure to call them.

"Legs . . . gone," Mello panted. "Can't feel nothing."

"Take it easy," Jim advised. The nearest place was Bill Katrishen's, and Bill might be some hand with a wounded man. He said as much to Mello. "Can't be more'n three, four miles," he added. "I'll give you back your gun and build up the fire."

"You . . . you'll sure come back?" Mello pleaded.

"What kind of coyote do you think I am?" Sandifer asked irritably. "I'll get back as soon as ever I can." He looked down at him. "Why were you gunning for me? Mont put you up to it?"

Mello shook his head. "Mont, he . . . he ain't . . . bad. It's that Martin . . . you watch. He's pizen mean."

Leaving the fire blazing brightly, Jim returned to his buckskin and jumped into the saddle. The moon was higher now, and the avenues through the trees were like roads, eerily lighted. Touching a spur to the horse, Jim raced through the night, the cool wind fanning his face. Once a deer scurried from in front of him and then bounded off through the trees, and once he thought he saw the lumbering shadow of an old grizzly.

The Katrishen log cabin and pole corrals lay bathed in white moonlight as he raced his horse into the yard. The drum of hoofs upon the hard-packed earth and his call brought movement and an answer from inside: "Who is it? What's up?"

Briefly he explained, and after a minute the door opened.

"Come in, Jim. Figured I heard a shot a while back. Dan Mello, you say? He's a bad one."

Hurrying to the corral, Jim harnessed two

mustangs and hitched them to the buckboard. A moment later Bill Katrishen, tall and gray-haired, came from the cabin, carrying a lantern in one hand and a black bag in the other.

"I'm no medical man," he said, "but I fixed a sight of bullet wounds in my time." He crawled into the buckboard, and one of his sons got up beside him.

Led by Sandifer, they started back over the way he had come.

Mello was still conscious when they stopped beside him. He looked unbelievingly at Katrishen.

"You came?" he said. "You knowed who . . . who I was?"

"You're hurt, ain't you?" Katrishen asked testily. Carefully he examined the man, and then sat back on his heels. "Mello," he said, "I ain't one for foolin' a man. You're plumb bad off. That bullet seems to have slid off your hip bone an' tore right through you. If we had you down to the house, we could work on you a durned sight better, but I don't know whether you'd make it or not."

The wounded man breathed heavily, staring from one to the other. He looked scared, and he was sweating, and under it his face was pale.

"What you think," he panted, "all right . . . with me."

"The three of us can put him on them quilts in

the back of the buckboard. Jim, you slide your hands under his back."

"Hold up." Mello's eyes wavered, and then focused on Jim. "You watch . . . Martin. He's plumb . . . bad."

"What's he want, Mello?" Jim said. "What's he after?"

"G . . . old," Mello panted, and then suddenly he relaxed.

"Fainted," Katrishen said. "Load him up."

All through the remainder of the night they worked over him. It was miles over mountain roads to Silver City and the nearest doctor, and little enough that he could do once he got there. Shortly before the sun lifted, Dan Mello died.

Bill Katrishen got up from beside the bed, his face drawn with weariness. He looked across the body of Dan Mello at Sandifer.

"Jim, what's this all about? Why was he gunning for you?"

Hesitating only a moment, Jim Sandifer explained the needling of Gray Bowen by Rose Martin, the undercover machinations of her and her tall son, the hiring of the Mellos at their instigation and of Art Dunn and Klee Mont. Then he went on to the events preceding his break with the B Bar. Katrishen nodded thoughtfully, but obviously puzzled.

"I never heard of the woman, Jim. I can't figure

why she'd have it in for me. What did Mello mean when he said Martin was after gold?"

"You've got me. I know they are money hungry, but the ranch is. . . ." He stopped, and his face lifted, his eyes narrowing. "Bill, did you ever hear of gold around here?"

"Sure, over toward Cooney Cañon. You know, Cooney was a sergeant in the Army, and after his discharge he returned to hunt for gold he located while a soldier. The Apaches finally got him, but he had gold first."

"Maybe that's it. I want a fresh horse, Bill."

"You get some sleep first. The boys an' I'll take care of Dan. Kara will fix breakfast for you."

The sun was high when Jim Sandifer rolled out of his bunk and stumbled sleepily to the door to splash his face in cold water poured from a bucket into the tin basin. Kara heard him moving and came to the door, walking carefully and lifting her hand to catch the doorjamb. "Hello, Jim? Are you rested? Dad and the boys buried Dan Mello over on the knoll."

Jim smiled at her reassuringly. "I'm rested, but after I eat, I'll be ridin', Kara." He looked up at the slender girl with the rusty hair and pale freckles. "You keep the boys in, will you? I don't want them to be where they could be shot at until I can figure a way out of this. I'm going to maintain peace in this country or die trying."

"You're a good man, Jim," the girl said. "This country needs more like you."

Sandifer shook his head somberly. "Not really a good man, Kara, just a man who wants peace and time to build a home. I reckon I've been as bad as most, but this is a country for freedom and a country for things to be done. We can't do it when we are killing each other."

The buckskin horse was resting, but the iron gray that Katrishen had provided was a good mountain horse. Jim Sandifer pulled his gray hat low over his eyes and squinted against the sun. He liked the smell of pine needles, the pungent smell of sage. He moved carefully, searching the trail for the way Lee Martin's horse had gone the day Grimes had followed him.

Twice he lost the trail and then found it only to lose it finally in the sand of a wash. The area covered by the sand was small, a place where water had spilled down a steep mountainside, eating out a raw wound in the cliff, yet there the trail vanished. Dismounting, Sandifer's careful search disclosed a brushed-over spot near the cliff and then a chafed spot near the cliff and then a chafed place on a small tree. Here Lee Martin had tied his horse, and from here he must have gone on foot.

It was a small rock, only half as big as his fist, that was the telltale clue. The rock showed where it had lain in the earth but had been recently rolled aside. Moving close, he could see that the stone had rolled from under a clump of brush; the clump rolled easily under his hand. Then he saw that, although the roots were still in the soil, at some time part of it had been pulled free, and the clump had been rolled over to cover an opening no more than a couple of feet wide and twice as high. It was a man-made tunnel, but one not recently made.

Concealing the gray in the trees some distance off, Sandifer walked back to the hole, stared around uneasily, and then ducked his head and entered. Once he was inside, the tunnel was higher and wider, and then it opened into a fair-size room. Here the ore had been stoped out, and he looked around, holding a match high. The light caught and glinted upon the rock, and moving closer he picked up a small chunk of rose quartz seamed with gold.

Pocketing the sample, he walked farther in until he saw a black hole, yawning before him, and beside it lay a notched pole such as the Indians had used in Spanish times to climb out of mine shafts. Looking over into the hole, he saw a longer pole reaching down into the darkness. He peered over, and then straightened. This, then, was what Dan Mello had meant. The Martins wanted gold.

The match flickered out, and, standing there in the cool darkness, he thought it over and understood. This place was on land used, and probably claimed, by Bill Katrishen, and it could not be worked unless he were driven off. But could Sandifer make Gray Bowen believe him? What would Lee do if his scheme was exposed? Why had Mello been so insistent that Martin was dangerous?

He bent over and started into the tunnel exit, and then stopped. Kneeling just outside were Lee Martin, Art Dunn, and Jay Mello. Lee had a shotgun pointed at Jim's body. Jim jerked back around the corner of stone even as the shotgun thundered.

"You dirty, murdering rat!" he yelled. "Let me out in the open and try that!"

Martin laughed. "I wouldn't think of it! You're right where I want you now, an' you'll stay there!"

Desperately Jim stared around. Martin was right. He was bottled up now. He drew his gun, wanting to chance a shot at Martin while yet there was time, but when he stole a glance around the corner of the tunnel, there was nothing to be seen. Suddenly he heard a sound of metal striking stone, a rattle of rock, and then a thunderous crash, and the tunnel was filled with dust, stifling and thick. Lee Martin had closed off the tunnel mouth, and he was entombed alive!

Jim Sandifer leaned back against the rock wall

of the stope and closed his eyes. He was frightened. He was frightened with a deep, soul-shaking fear, for this was something against which he could not fight, these walls of living rock around him, and the dead débris of the rock-choked tunnel. Had there been time and air, a man might work out an escape, but there was so little time, so little air. He was buried alive.

Slowly the dust settled from the heavy air. Saving his few matches, he got down on his knees and crawled into the tunnel, but there was barely room enough. Mentally he tried to calculate the distance out, and he could see that there was no less than fifteen feet of rock between him and escape—not an impossible task if more rock did not slide down from above. Remembering the mountain, he knew that above the tunnel mouth it was almost one vast slide. He could hear nothing, and the air was hot and close.

On his knees he began to feel his way around, crawling until he reached the tunnel and the notched pole. Here he hesitated, wondering what the darkness below would hold. Water, perhaps? Or even snakes? He had heard of snakes taking over old mines, and once, crawling down the ladder into an old shaft, he had seen an enormous rattler, the biggest he had ever seen, coiled about the ladder just below him. Nevertheless, he began to descend—down, down into the abysmal blackness below him. He seemed to have climbed down an interminable distance when suddenly his boot touched rock.

Standing upright, one hand on the pole, he reached out. His hand found rock on three sides, on the other only empty space. He turned in that direction and ran smack into the rock wall, knocking sparks from his skull. He drew back, swearing, and found the tunnel. At the same time, his hand touched something else, a sort of ledge in the corner of the rock, and on the ledge—his heart gave a leap. Candles!

Quickly he got out a match and lit the first one. Then he walked into the tunnel. Here was more of the rose quartz, and it was incredibly seamed with gold. Lee Martin had made a strike. Rather, studying the walls, he had perhaps found an old Spanish working, although work had been done here within the last few weeks. Suddenly Jim saw a pick and he grinned. There might yet be a way out. Yet a few minutes of exploration sufficed to indicate that there was no other opening. If he was to go out, it must be by the way he came.

Taking the candles with him, he climbed the notched pole and stuck a lighted candle on a rock. Then, with a pick at his side, he started to work at the débris choking the tunnel. He lifted a rock and moved it aside, then another.

An hour later, soaked with sweat, he was still working away, pausing each minute or so to examine the hanging wall. The tunnel was cramped, and the work moved slowly ahead, for every stone removed had to be shoved back into the stope behind him. He reached the broken part overhead and, when he moved a rock, more slid down. He worked on, his breath coming in great gasps, sweat dripping from his face and neck to his hands.

A new sound came to him, a faint tapping. He held still, listening, trying to quiet his breathing and the pound of his heart. Then he heard it again, an unmistakable tapping!

Grasping his pick, he tapped three times, then an interval, then three times again. Then he heard somebody pull at the rocks of the tunnel, and his heart pounded with exultation. He had been found!

How the following hours passed Sandifer never quite knew, but, working feverishly, he fought his way through the border of time that divided him from the outer world and the clean, pine-scented air. Suddenly a stone was moved and an arrow of light stabbed the darkness, and with it came the cool air he wanted. He took a deep breath, filling his lungs with air so liquid it might almost be water, and then he went to work, helping the hands outside to enlarge the opening. When there was room enough, he thrust his head and shoulders through and then pulled himself out and stood up, dusting himself off—and found he was facing not Bill Katrishen or one of his sons, but Jay Mello!

"You?" he was astonished. "What brought you back?"

Jay wiped his thick hands on his jeans and looked uncomfortable.

"Never figured to bury no man alive," he said. "That was Martin's idea. Anyway, Katrishen told me what you done for Dan."

"Did he tell you I'd killed him? I'm sorry, Jay. It was him or me."

"Sure. I knowed that when he come after you. I didn't like it nohow. What I meant, well . . . you could've left him lie. You didn't need to go git help for him. I went huntin' Dan, when I found you was alive, an' I figured it was like that, that he was dead. Katrishen gave me his clothes, an' I found this. . . ."

It was a note, scrawled painfully, perhaps on a rifle stock or a flat rock, written no doubt, while Jim was gone for help.

Jay

Git shet of Marten. Sandfer's all right. He's gone for hulp to Katrisshn. I'm hard hit. Sandfer shore is wite. So long, Jay, good ridin.

Dan

"I'm sorry, Jay. He was game."

"Sure." Jay Mello scowled. "It was Martin got us into this, him an' Klee Mont. We never done no killin' before . . . maybe stole a few hosses or run off a few head of cows."

"What's happened? How long was I in there?" Jim glanced at the sun.

"About five, six hours. She'll be dark soon." Mello hesitated. "I reckon I'm goin' to take out . . . light a shuck for Texas."

Sandifer thrust out his hand. "Good luck, Jay. Maybe we'll meet again."

The outlaw nodded. He stared at the ground, and then he looked up, his tough, unshaven face strangely lonely in the late-afternoon sun. "Sure wish Dan was ridin' with me. We always rode together, him an' me, since we was kids." He rubbed a hard hand over his lips. "What d'you know? That girl back to Katrishen's? She put some flowers on his grave. Sure enough."

He turned and walked to his horse, swung into the saddle, and walked his horse down the trail, a somber figure captured momentarily by the sunlight before he turned away under the pines. Incongruously Jim noticed that the man's vest was split up the back, and the crown of his hat was torn.

The gray waited patiently by the brush. Jim Sandifer untied him and swung into the saddle. It was a fast ride he made back to the ranch on Iron

Creek. There he swapped saddles, explaining all to Katrishen. "I'm riding," he said. "There's no room in this country for Lee Martin now."

"Want us to come?" Bill asked.

"No. They might think it was war. You stay out of it, for we want no Pleasant Valley War here. Leave it lay. I'll settle this."

He turned from the trail before he reached the B Bar, riding through the cottonwoods and sycamores along the creek. Then he rode up between the buildings and stopped beside the corral. The saddle leather creaked when he swung down, and he saw a slight movement at the corner of the corral.

"Klee? Is that you?" It was Art Dunn. "What's goin' on up at the house?"

Jim Sandifer took a long step forward. "No, Art," he said swiftly, "it's me."

Dunn took a quick step back and grabbed for his gun, but Jim was already moving, expecting him to reach. Sandifer's left hand dropped to Art's wrist, and his right smashed up in a wicked uppercut to the solar plexus.

Dunn grunted and his knees sagged. Jim let go of his wrist then, and hooked sharply to the chin, hearing Dunn's teeth click as the blow smashed home. Four times more Jim hit him, rocking his head on his shoulders, then he smashed another punch to the wind and, grabbing Dunn's belt buckle, jerked his gun belt open. The belt slipped down and Dunn staggered and went to his knees. The outlaw pawed wildly, trying to get at Jim, but he was still gasping for the wind that had been knocked out of him.

The bunkhouse door opened and Sparkman stepped into the light. "What's the matter?" he asked. "What goes on?"

Sandifer called softly, and Sparkman grunted and came down off the steps. "Jim? You here? There's the devil to pay up at the house, man. I don't know what came off up there, but there was a shootin'! When we tried to go up, Mont was on the steps with a shotgun to drive us back."

"Take care of this *hombre*. I'll find out what's wrong fast enough. Where's Grimes an' Rep?"

"Rep Dean rode over to the line cabin on Cabin Creek to round up some boys in case of trouble. Grimes is inside."

"Then take Dunn an' keep your eyes open. I may need help. If I yell, come loaded for bear and hunting hair."

Jim Sandifer turned swiftly and started for the house. He walked rapidly, circling as he went toward the little-used front door, opened only on company occasions. That door, he knew, opened into a large, old-fashioned parlor that was rarely used. It was a show place, stiff and uncomfortable, and mostly gilt and plush. The front door was usually locked, but he remembered that he had occasion to help move some furniture not long before and the door had been left unlocked. There was every chance that it still was, for the room was so little used as to be almost forgotten.

Easing up on the verandah, he tiptoed across to the door and gently turned the knob. The door opened inward, and he stepped swiftly through and closed it behind him. All was dark and silent, but there was light under the intervening door and a sound of movement. With the thick carpet muffling his footfalls, he worked his way across the room to the door.

"How's the old man?" Martin was asking.

His mother replied. "He's all right. He'll live."

Martin swore. "If that girl hadn't bumped me, I'd have killed him and we'd be better off. We could easy enough fix things so that Sandifer would get blamed for it."

"Don't be in such a hurry," Rose Martin intervened. "You're always in such a fret. The girl's here, an' we can use her to help. As long as we have her, the old man will listen, and, while he's hurt, she'll do as she's told."

Martin muttered under his breath. "If we'd started by killing Sandifer like I wanted, all would be well," he said irritably. "What he said about the Katrishen trouble startin' with our comin' got the old man to thinkin'. Then I figure Bowen was sorry he fired his foreman."

"No matter." Rose Martin was brusque.

"We've got this place, and we can handle the Katrishens ourselves. There's plenty of time now Sandifer's gone."

Steps sounded. "Lee, the old man's comin' out of it. He wants his daughter."

"Tell him to go climb a tree," Martin replied stiffly. "You watch him."

"Where's Art?" Klee protested. "I don't like it, Lee. He's been gone too long. Somethin's up."

"*Aw,* forget it. Quit cryin'. You do more yelpin' than a mangy coyote."

Sandifer stood very still, thinking. There was no sound of Elaine, so she must be a prisoner in her room. Turning, he tiptoed across the room toward the far side. A door there, beyond the old piano, opened into Elaine's room. Carefully he tried the knob. It held.

At that very instant a door opened abruptly, and he saw light under the door before him. He heard a startled gasp from Elaine and Lee Martin's voice, taunting, familiar.

"What's the matter? Scared?" Martin laughed. "I just came in to see if you was all right. If you'd kept that pretty mouth of yours shut, your dad would still be all right. You tellin' him Sandifer was correct about the Katrishens an' that he shouldn't've fired him. . . ."

"He shouldn't have," the girl said quietly. "If he was here now, he'd kill you. Get out of my room."

85

"Maybe I ain't ready to go," he taunted. "An' from now on I'm goin to come an' go as I like."

His steps advanced into the room, and Jim tightened his grip on the knob. He remembered that lock, and it was not set very securely. Suddenly an idea came to him. Turning, he picked up an old glass lamp, large and ornate. Balancing it momentarily in his hand, he drew it back and hurled it with a long overhand swing through the window.

Glass crashed on the verandah, and the lamp hit, went down a step, and stayed there. Inside the girl's room, there was a startled exclamation, and he heard running footsteps from both the girl's room and the old man's. Somebody yelled: "What's that? What happened?" And he hurled his shoulder against the door.

As he had expected, the flimsy lock carried away and he was catapulted through the door into Elaine's bedroom. Catching himself, he wheeled like a cat and sprang for the door that opened into the living room beyond. He reached it just as Mont jerked the curtain back, but, not wanting to endanger the girl, he swung hard with his fist instead of drawing his gun.

The blow came out of a clear sky to smash Mont on the jaw, and he staggered back into the room. Jim Sandifer sprang through, legs spread, hands wide.

"You, Martin," he said sharply. "Draw!"

Lee Martin was a killer, but no gunman. White to the lips, his eyes deadly, he sprang behind his mother and grabbed for the shotgun.

"Shoot, Jim!" Elaine cried. "Shoot!"

He could not. Rose Martin stood between him and his target, and Martin had the shotgun now and was swinging it. Jim lunged, shoving the table over, and the lamp shattered in a crash. He fired, and then fired again. Flame stabbed the darkness at him, and he fell back against the wall, switching his gun. Fire laced the darkness into a stabbing crimson crossfire, and the room thundered with sound, and then died to stillness that was the stillness of death itself.

No sound remained, only the acrid smell of gunpowder mingled with the smell of coal oil and the faint, sickish-sweet smell of blood. His guns ready, Jim crouched in the darkness, alert for movement. Somebody groaned, and then sighed deeply, and a spur grated on the floor. From the next room, Gray Bowen called weakly: "Daughter? Daughter, what's happened? What's wrong?"

There was no movement yet, but the darkness grew more familiar. Jim's eyes became more accustomed to it. He could see no one standing. Yet it was Elaine who broke the stillness.

"Jim? Jim, are you all right? Oh, Jim . . . are you safe?" Maybe they were waiting for this.

"I'm all right," he said.

"Light your lamp, will you?"

Deliberately he moved, and there was no sound within the room, only outside, a running of feet on the hard-packed earth. Then a door slammed open, and Sparkman stood there, gun in hand.

"It's all right, I think," Sandifer said. "We shot it out."

Elaine entered the room with a light and caught herself with a gasp at the sight before her. Jim reached for the lamp.

"Go to your father," he said swiftly. "We'll take care of this."

Sparkman looked around, and was followed into the room by Grimes. "Good grief," he gasped. "They are all dead. All of them."

"The woman, too?" Sandifer's face paled. "I hope I didn't. . . ."

"You didn't," Grimes said. "She was shot in the back by her own son. Shootin' in the dark, blind an' gun crazy."

"Maybe it's better," Sparkman said. "She was an old hellion."

Klee Mont had caught his right at the end of his eyebrow, and a second shot along the ribs. Sandifer walked away from him and stood over Lee Martin. His face twisted in a sneer, the dead man lay sprawled on the floor, literally shot to doll rags.

"You didn't miss many," Sparkman said grimly.

"I didn't figure to," Jim said. "I'll see the old man, and then give you a hand."

"Forget it." Grimes looked up, his eyes faintly humorous. "You stay in there. An' don't spend all your time with the old man. We need a new set-up on this here spread, an' with a new son-in-law who's a first-rate cattleman, Gray could set back an' relax."

Sandifer stopped with his hand on the curtain. "Maybe you got something there," he said thoughtfully. "Maybe you have."

"You can take my word for it," Elaine said, stepping into the door beside Jim. "He has. He surely has."

FOUR CARD DRAW

When a man drew four cards, he could expect something like this to happen. Ben Taylor had probably been right when he told him his luck had run out. Despite that, he had a place of his own and, come what may, he was going to keep it.

Nor was there any fault to find with the place. From the moment Allen Ring rode his claybank into the valley he knew he was coming home. This was it; this was the place. Here he would stop. He'd been tumbleweeding all over the West now for ten years, and it was time he stopped if he ever did, and this looked like his fence corner.

Even the cabin looked good, although Taylor told him the place had been empty for three years. It looked solid and fit, and, while the grass was waist high all over the valley and up around the house, he could see trails through it, some of them made by unshod ponies, that meant wild horses, and some by deer. Then there were the tracks of a single shod horse, always the same one.

Those tracks always led right up to the door, and they stopped there; yet he could see that somebody with mighty small feet had been walking up to peer into the windows. Why would a person want to look into a window more than once? The window of an empty cabin? He had gone up and looked in himself, and all he saw was a dusty, dark interior with a ray of light from the opposite window, a table, a couple of chairs, and a fine old fireplace that had been built by skilled hands.

"You never built that fireplace, Ben Taylor," Ring had muttered, "you who never could handle anything but a running iron or a deck of cards. You never built anything in your life as fine and useful as that."

The cabin sat on a low ledge of grass backed up against the towering cliff of red rock, and the spring was not more than fifty feet away, a stream that came out of the rock and trickled pleasantly into a small basin before spilling out and winding thoughtfully down the valley to join a larger stream, a quarter of a mile away.

There were some tall spruces around the cabin, and a couple of sycamores and a cottonwood near the spring. Some gooseberry bushes, too, and a couple of apple trees. The trees had been pruned.

"And you never did that, either, Ben Taylor," Allen Ring had said soberly. "I wish I knew more about this place."

Time had fled like a scared antelope, and with

the scythe he found in the pole barn he cut off the tall grass around the house, patched up the holes in the cabin where the pack rats had got in, and even thinned out the bushes—it had been several years since they had been touched—and repaired the pole barn.

The day he picked to clean out the spring was the day Gail Truman rode up to the house. He had been putting the finishing touches on a chair bottom he was making when he heard a horse's hoof strike stone, and he straightened up to see the girl sitting on the red pony. She was staring, open-mouthed, at the stacked hay from the grass he had cut and the washed windows of the house. He saw her swing down and run up to the window, and dropping his tools he strolled up.

"Hunting somebody, ma'am?"

She wheeled and stared at him, her wide blue eyes accusing. "What are you doing here?" she demanded. "What do you mean by moving in like this?"

He smiled, but he was puzzled, too. Ben Taylor had said nothing about a girl, especially a girl like this. "Why, I own the place?" he said. "I'm fixing it up so's I can live here."

"You own it?" Her voice was incredulous, agonized. "You couldn't own it! You couldn't. The man who owns this place is gone, and he would never sell it. Never!"

"He didn't exactly sell it, ma'am," Ring said

gently. "He lost it to me in a poker game. That was down Texas way."

She was horrified. "In a poker game? Whit Bayly in a poker game? I don't believe it!"

"The man I won it from was called Ben Taylor, ma'am." Ring took the deed from his pocket and opened it. "Come to think of it, Ben did say that, if anybody asked about Whit Bayly, to say that he died down in the Guadaloupes . . . of lead poisoning."

"Whit Bayly is dead?" The girl looked stunned. "You're sure? Oh."

Her face went white and still and something in it seemed to die. She turned with a little gesture of despair and stared out across the valley, and his eyes followed hers. It was strange, Allen Ring told himself, but it was the first time he had looked just that way, and he stood there, caught up by something nameless, some haunting sense of the familiar.

Before him lay the tall grass of the valley, turning slightly now with the brown of autumn, and to his right a dark stand of spruce, standing stiffly, like soldiers on parade, and beyond them the swell of the hill, and farther to the right the hill rolled up and stopped, and beyond lay a wider valley fading away into the vast purple and mauve of distance and here and there spotted with the golden candles of cottonwoods, their leaves bright yellow with nearing cold.

There was no word for this; it was a picture, yet a picture of which a man could only dream and never reproduce.

"It . . . it's beautiful, isn't it?" he said.

She turned on him, and for the first time she seemed really to look at him, a tall young man with a shock of rust-brown hair and somber gray eyes, having about him the look of a rider and the look of a lonely man.

"Yes, it is beautiful. Oh, I've come here so many times to see it, the cabin, too. I think this is the loveliest place I have ever seen. I used to dream about. . . ." She stopped, suddenly confused. "Oh, I'm sorry. I shouldn't talk so." She looked at him soberly. "I'd better go. I guess this is yours now."

He hesitated. "Ma'am," he said sincerely, "the place is mine, and, sure enough, I love it. I wouldn't swap this place for anything. But that view, that belongs to no man. It belongs to whoever looks at it with eyes to see it, so you come any time you like, and look all you please." Ring grinned. "Fact is," he said, "I'm aiming to fix the place up inside, and I'm sure no hand at such things. Maybe you could sort of help me. I'd like it kind of homey-like." He flushed. "You see, I sort of lived in bunkhouses all my life and never had no such place."

She smiled with a quick understanding and sympathy. "Of course! I'd love to, only . . ."—her face sobered—"you won't be able to stay here. You haven't seen Ross Bilton yet, have you?"

"Who's he?" Ring asked curiously. He nodded toward the horsemen he saw approaching. "Is this the one?"

She turned quickly and nodded. "Be careful. He's the town marshal. The men with him are Ben Hagen and Stan Brule."

Brule he remembered—but would Brule remember him?

"By the way, my name is Allen Ring," he said, low-voiced.

"I'm Gail Truman. My father owns the Tall T brand."

Bilton was a big man with a white hat. Ring decided he didn't like him and that the feeling was going to be mutual. Brule he knew, so the stocky man was Ben Hagen. Brule had changed but little, some thinner, maybe, but his hatchet face as lean and poisonous as always.

"How are you, Gail?" Bilton said briefly. "Is this a friend of yours?"

Allen Ring liked to get his cards on the table. "Yes, a friend of hers, but also the owner of this place."

"You own Red Rock?" Bilton was incredulous. "That will be very hard to prove, my friend. Also, this place is under the custody of the law."

"Whose law?" Ring wanted to know. He was

aware that Brule was watching him, wary but uncertain as yet.

"Mine. I'm the town marshal. There was a murder committed here, and until that murder is solved and the killer brought to justice, this place will not he touched. You have already seen fit to make changes, but perhaps the court will be lenient."

"You're the town marshal?" Allen Ring shoved his hat back on his head and reached for his tobacco. "That's mighty interesting. Howsoever, let me remind you that you're out of town right now."

"That makes no difference." Bilton's voice was sharp. Ring could see that he was not accustomed to being told off, that his orders were usually obeyed. "You will get off this place before nightfall."

"It makes a sight of difference to me," Allen replied calmly. "I bought this place by staking everything I had against it in a poker game. I drew four cards to win, a nine to match one I had and three aces. It was a fool play that paid off. I registered the deed. She's mine, legal. I know of no law that allows a place to be kept idle because there was a murder committed on it. If after all this time it hasn't been solved, I suggest the town get a new marshal."

Ross Bilton was angry, but he kept himself under control. "I've warned you, and you've been told to leave. If you do not leave, I'll use my authority to move you."

Ring smiled. "Now, listen, Bilton. You might pull that stuff on some folks that don't like trouble. You might bluff somebody into believing you had the authority to do this. You don't bluff me, and I simply don't scare . . . do I, Brule?"

He turned on Brule so sharply that the man stiffened in his saddle, his hand poised as though to grab for a gun. The half-breed's face stiffened with irritation, and then recognition came to him. "Allen Ring," he said. "You again."

"That's right, Brule. Only this time I'm not taking cattle through the Indian Nation. Not pushing them by that ratty bunch of rustlers and highbinders you rode with." Ring turned his eyes toward Bilton. "You're the law? And you ride with him? Why, the man's wanted in every county in Texas for everything from murder to horse thieving."

Ross Bilton stared at Ring for a long minute. "You've been warned," he said.

"And I'm staying," Ring replied sharply. "And keep your coyotes away if you come again. I don't like 'em."

Brule's fingers spread and his lips stiffened with cold fury. Ring watched him calmly. "You know better than that, Brule. Wait until my back is turned. If you reach for a gun, I'll blow you out of your saddle."

Stan Brule slowly relaxed his hand, and then wordlessly he turned to follow Bilton and Hagen, who had watched with hard eyes.

Gail Truman was looking at him curiously. "Why, Brule was afraid of you!" she exclaimed. "Who are you, anyway?"

"Nobody, ma'am," he said simply. "I'm no gunfighter, just an *hombre* who ain't got brains enough to scare proper. Brule knows it. He knows he might beat me, but he knows I'd kill him. He was there when I killed a friend of his, Blaze Garden."

"But . . . but then you must be a gunman. Blaze Garden was a killer. I've heard Dad and the boys talk about him."

"No, I'm no gunman. Blaze beat me to the draw. In fact, he got off his first shot before my gun cleared the holster, only he shot too quick and missed. His second and third shots hit me while I was walking into him. The third shot wasn't so bad because I was holding my fire and getting close. He got scared and stepped back, and the fourth shot was too high. Then I shot and I was close up to him then. One was enough. One is always enough if you place it right." He gestured at the place. "What's this all about? Mind telling me?"

"It's very simple, really. Nothing out here is very involved when you come to that. It seems that there's something out here that brings men to using guns much faster than in other places, and one thing stems from another. Whit Bayly owned this place. He was a fixing man, always tinkering and fixing things up. He was a tall, handsome man who all the girls loved. . . ."

"You, too?" he asked quizzically.

She flushed. "Yes, I guess so, only I'm only eighteen now, and that was three, almost four years ago. I wasn't very pretty or very noticeable and much too young. Sam Hazlitt was one of the richest men in the country around here, and Whit had a run-in with him over a horse. There had been a lot of stealing going on around, and Hazlitt traced some stock of his to this ranch, or so he claimed. Anyway, he accused Bayly of it, and Whit told him not to talk foolish. Furthermore, he told Hazlitt to stay off of his ranch. Well, folks were divided over who was in the right, but Whit had a lot of friends and Hazlitt had four brothers and clannish as all get out.

"Not long after, some riders from Buck Hazlitt's ranch came by that way and saw a body lying in the yard, right over near the spring. When they came down to have a look, thinking Whit was hurt, they found Sam Hazlitt, and he'd been shot dead . . . in the back. They headed right for town, hunting Whit, and they found him. He denied it, and they were going to hang him, had a rope around his neck, and then I . . . I . . . well, I

100

swore he wasn't anywhere near his ranch all day."

"It wasn't true?" Ring asked keenly, his eyes searching the girl's face. She avoided his eyes, flushing even more.

"Not . . . not exactly. But I knew he wasn't guilty. I just knew he wouldn't shoot a man in the back. I told them he was over to our place, talking with me, and he hadn't time to get back there and kill Sam. Folks didn't like it much. Some of them still believed he killed Sam, and some didn't like it because, despite the way I said it, they figured he was sparking a girl too young for him. I always said it wasn't that. As a matter of fact, I did see Whit over our way, but the rest of it was lies. Anyway, after a few weeks Whit up and left the country."

"I see, and nobody knows yet who killed Sam Hazlitt?"

"Nobody. One thing that was never understood was what became of Sam's account book . . . sort of a tally book, but more than that. It was a sort of record he kept of a lot of things, and it was gone out of his pocket. Nobody ever found it, but they did find the pencil Sam used on the sand nearby. Dad always figured Sam lived long enough to write something, but that the killer stole the book and destroyed it."

"How about the hands? Could they have picked it up? Did Bilton question them about that?"

"Oh, Bilton wasn't marshal then. In fact, he

was riding for Buck Hazlitt then. He was one of the hands who found Sam's body."

After the girl had gone, Allen Ring walked back to the house and thought the matter over. He had no intention of leaving. This was just the ranch he wanted, and he intended to live right here, yet the problem fascinated him. Living in the house and looking around the place had taught him a good deal about Whit Bayly. He was, as Gail had said, "a fixing man" for there were many marks of his handiwork aside from the beautifully made fireplace and the pruned apple trees. He was, Ring was willing to gamble, no murderer.

Taylor had said he died of lead poisoning. Who had killed Bayly? Why? Was it a casual shooting over some rangeland argument, or had he been followed from here by someone on vengeance bent? Or someone who thought he might know too much?

"You'll like the place." Taylor had said—that was an angle he hadn't considered before. Ben Taylor had actually seen this place himself! The more sign he read, the more tricky the trail became, and Allen walked outside and sat down against the cabin wall when his supper was finished, and lighted a smoke.

Stock had been followed to the ranch by Sam Hazlitt. If Whit was not the thief, then who was? Where had the stock been driven? He turned his eyes almost automatically toward the Mogollons, the logical place. His eyes narrowed, and he recalled that one night while playing cards they had been talking of springs and water holes, and Ben Taylor had talked about Fossil Springs, a huge spring that roared thousands of gallons of water out of the earth.

"Place a man could run plenty of stock," he had said, and winked, "and nobody the wiser."

Those words had been spoken far away and long ago, and the Red Rock ranch had not yet been put on the table; that was months later. There was, he recalled, a Fossil Creek somewhere north of here. And Fossil Creek might flow from Fossil Springs—perhaps Ben Taylor had talked more to effect than he knew. That had been Texas, and this was Arizona, and a casual bunkhouse conversation probably seemed harmless enough.

"We'll see, Ben," Ring muttered grimly. "We'll see."

Ross Bilton had been one of the Hazlitt hands at the time of the killing, one of the first on the scene. Now he was town marshal but interested in keeping the ranch unoccupied—why? None of it made sense, yet actually it was no business of his. Allen Ring thought that over and decided it was his business in a sense. He now owned the place and lived on it. If an old murder was to interfere with his living there, it behooved him to know the facts. It was a slight excuse for his curiosity.

Morning came and the day drew on toward noon, and there was no sign of Bilton or Brule. Ring had loaded his rifle and kept it close to hand, and he was wearing two guns, thinking he might need a loaded spare, although he rarely wore more than one. Also, inside the cabin door he had his double-barreled shotgun.

The spring drew his attention. At the moment he did not wish to leave the vicinity of the cabin, and that meant it was a good time to clean out the spring. Not that it needed it, but there were loose stones in the bottom of the basin and some moss. With this removed, he would have more water and clearer water. With a wary eye toward the cañon mouth, he began his work.

The sound of an approaching horse drew him erect. His rifle stood against the rocks at hand, and his guns were ready, yet, as the rider came into sight, he saw there was only one man, a stranger. He rode a fine bay gelding and he was not a young man, but thick and heavy with drooping mustache and kind blue eyes. He drew up.

"Howdy," he said affably, yet taking a quick glance around before looking again at Ring. "I'm Rolly Truman, Gail's father."

"It's a pleasure," Ring said, wiping his wet hands on a red bandanna. "Nice to know the neighbors." He nodded at the spring. "I picked me a job. That hole's deeper than it looks."

"Good flow of water," Truman agreed. He chewed his mustache thoughtfully. "I like to see a young man with get-up about him, startin' his own spread, willin' to work."

Allen Ring waited. The man was building up to something; what, he knew not. It came then, carefully at first, yet shaping a loop as it drew near. "Not much range here, of course," Truman added. "You should have more graze. Ever been over in Cedar Basin? Or up along the East Verde bottom? Wonderful land up there, still some wild, but a country where a man could really do something with a few white-faced cattle."

"No, I haven't seen it," Ring replied, "but I'm satisfied. I'm not land hungry. All I want is a small piece, and this suits me fine."

Truman shifted in his saddle and looked uncomfortable. "Fact is, son, you're upsetting a lot of folks by being here. What you should do is move."

"I'm sorry," Ring said flatly. "I don't want to make enemies, but I won this place on a four card draw. Maybe I'm a fatalist, but somehow or other I think I should stick here. No man's got a right to think he can draw four cards and win anything, but I did, and in a plenty rough game. I had everything I owned in that pot. Now I got the place."

The rancher sat his horse uneasily, and then he shook his head. "Son, you've sure got to move. There's no trouble here now, but if you stay, she's liable to open old sores and start more trouble than any of us can stop. Besides, how did Ben Taylor get title to this place? Bayly had no love for him. I doubt if your title will stand up in court."

"As to that I don't know," Ring persisted stubbornly. "I have a deed that's legal enough, and I've registered that deed and my brand along with it. I did find out that Bayly had no heirs. So I reckon I'll sit tight until somebody comes along with a better legal claim than mine."

Truman ran his hand over his brow. "Well, I guess I don't blame you much, son. Maybe I shouldn't have come over, but I know Ross Bilton and his crowd, and I reckon I wanted to save myself some trouble as well as you. Gail, she thinks you're a fine young man. In fact, you're the first man she's ever showed interest in since Whit left, and she was a youngster then. It was a sort of hero worship she had for him. I don't want trouble."

Allen Ring leaned on the shovel and looked up at the older man. "Truman," he said, "are you sure you aren't buying trouble by trying to avoid it? Just what's your stake in this?"

The rancher sat very still, his face drawn and pale. Then he got down from his horse and sat on a rock. Removing his hat, he mopped his brow.

"Son," he said slowly, "I reckon I got to trust you. You've heard of the Hazlitts. They are a hard, clannish bunch, men who've lived by the gun most of their lives. Sam was murdered. Folks all know that when they find out who murdered him and why, there's goin' to be plenty of trouble around here. Plenty."

"Did you kill him?"

Truman jerked his head up. "No! No, you mustn't get that idea, but . . . well, you know how small ranchers are. There was a sight of rustlin' them days, and the Hazlitts were the big outfit. They lost cows."

"And some of them got your brand?" Ring asked shrewdly.

Truman nodded. "I reckon. Not so many, though. And not only me. Don't get me wrong, I'm not beggin' off the blame. Part of it is mine, all right, but I didn't get many. Eight or ten of us hereabouts slapped brands on Hazlitt stock . . . and at least five of us have the biggest brands around here now, some as big almost as the Hazlitts'."

Allen Ring studied the skyline thoughtfully. It was an old story and one often repeated in the West. When the War Between the States ended, men came home to Texas and the Southwest to find cattle running in thousands, unbranded and unowned. The first man to slap on a brand was the owner, with no way he could be contested.

Many men grew rich with nothing more than a wide loop and a running iron. Then the unbranded cattle were gone, the ranches had settled into going concerns, and the great days of casual branding had ended, yet there was still free range, and a man with that same loop and running iron could still build a herd fast.

More than one of the biggest ranchers had begun that way, and many of them continued to brand loose stock wherever found. No doubt that had been true here, and these men like Rolly Truman, good, able men who had fought Indians and built their homes to last, had begun just that way. Now the range was mostly fenced, and ranches had narrowed somewhat, but Ring could see what it might mean to open an old sore now.

Sam Hazlitt had been trailing rustlers—he had found out who they were and where the herds were taken, and he had been shot down from behind. The catch was that the tally book, with his records, was still missing. That tally book might contain evidence as to the rustling done by men who were now pillars of the community and open them to the vengeance of the Hazlitt outfit.

Often Western men threw a blanket over a situation. If a rustler had killed Sam, then all the rustlers involved would be equally guilty. Anyone who lived on this ranch might stumble on that tally book and throw the range into a bloody gun war in which many men now beyond the errors of their youth, with homes, families, and different customs, would die.

It could serve no purpose to blow the lid off the trouble now, yet Allen Ring had a hunch. In their fear of trouble for themselves they might be concealing an even greater crime, aiding a murderer in his escape. There were lines of care in the face of Rolly Truman that a settled, established rancher should not have.

"Sorry," Ring said, "I'm staying. I like this place."

All through the noon hour the tension was building. The air was warm and sultry, and there was a thickening haze over the mountains. There was that hot thickness in the air that presaged a storm. When he left his coffee to return to work, Ring saw three horsemen coming into the cañon mouth at a running walk. He stopped in the door and touched his lips with his tongue.

They reined up at the door, three hard-bitten, hard-eyed men with rifles across their saddle bows. Men with guns in their holsters and men of a kind that would never turn from trouble. These were men with the bark on, lean fanatics with lips thinned with old bitterness.

The older man spoke first. "Ring, I've heard about you. I'm Buck Hazlitt. These are my brothers, Joe and Dolph. There's talk around that you aim to stay on this place. There's been talk for years that Sam hid his tally book here. We figure the killer got that book and burned it. Maybe he did, and, again, maybe not. We want that book. If you want to stay on this place, you stay. But if you find that book, you bring it to us."

Ring looked from one to the other, and he could see the picture clearly. With men like these, hard and unforgiving, it was no wonder Rolly Truman and the other ranchers were worried. The years and prosperity had eased Rolly and his like into comfort and softness, but not these. The Hazlitts were of feudal blood and background.

"Hazlitt," Ring said, "I know how you feel. You lost a brother, and that means something, but if that book is still around, which I doubt, and I find it, I'll decide what to do with it all by myself. I don't aim to start a range war. Maybe there's some things best forgotten. The man who murdered Sam Hazlitt ought to pay."

"We'll handle that," Dolph put in grimly. "You find that book, you bring it to us. If you don't. . . ." His eyes hardened. "Well, we'd have to class you with the crooks."

Ring's eyes shifted to Dolph. "Class if you want," he flared. "I'll do what seems best to me with that book. But all of you folks are plumb proddy over that tally book. Chances are nine out of ten the killer found it and destroyed it."

"I don't reckon he did," Buck said coldly, "because we know he's been back here, a-huntin' it. Him an' his girl."

Ring stiffened. "You mean . . . ?"

"What we mean is our figger, not yours." Buck Hazlitt reined his horse around. "You been told. You bring that book to us. You try to buck the Hazlitts and you won't stay in this country."

Ring had his back up. Despite himself he felt cold anger mounting within him. "Put this in your pipe, friend," he said harshly. "I came here to stay. No Hazlitt will change that. I ain't hunting trouble, but if you bring trouble to me, I'll handle it. I can bury a Hazlitt as easy as any other man."

Not one of them condescended to notice the remark. Turning their horses, they walked them down the cañon and out of it into the sultry afternoon. Allen Ring mopped the sweat from his face and listened to the deep rumbling of far-off thunder, growling among the cañons like a grizzly with a toothache. It was going to rain. Sure as shooting, it was going to rain—a regular gully washer.

There was yet time to finish the job on the spring, so he picked up his shovel and started back for the job. The rock basin was nearly cleaned and he finished removing the few rocks and the moss that had gathered. Then he opened the escape channel a little more to insure a more rapid emptying and filling process in the basin into which the trickle of water fell.

The water emerged from a crack in the rocks and trickled into the basin, and, finishing his job, Ring glanced thoughtfully to see if anything remained undone. There was still some moss on the rocks from which the water flowed, and, kneeling down, he leaned over to scrape it away. Pulling away the last shreds, he noticed a space from which a rock had recently fallen. Pulling more moss away, he dislodged another rock, and there, pushed into a niche, was a small black book!

Sam Hazlitt, dying, had evidently managed to shove it back in this crack in the rocks, hoping it would be found by someone not the killer.

Sitting back on his haunches, Ring opened the faded, canvas-bound book. A flap crossed over the page ends, and the book had been closed by a small tongue that slid into a loop of the canvas cover. Opening the book, he saw the pages were stained, but still legible.

The next instant he was struck by lightning. At least, that was what seemed to happen. Thunder crashed, and something struck him on the skull and he tried to rise and something struck again. He felt a drop of rain on his face and his eyes opened wide, and then another blow caught him and he faded out into darkness, his fingers clawing at the grass to keep from slipping down into that velvety, smothering blackness.

• • •

He was wet. He turned a little, lying there, thinking he must have left a window open and the rain was. . . . His eyes opened and he felt rain pounding on his face and he stared, not at a boot with a California spur, but at dead brown grass, soaked with rain now, and the glistening smoothness of water-worn stones. He was soaked to the hide.

Struggling to his knees, he looked around, his head heavy, his lips and tongue thick. He blinked at a gray, rain-slanted world and at low gray clouds and a distant rumble of thunder following a streak of lightning along the mountaintops.

Lurching to his feet, he stumbled toward the cabin and pitched over the doorsill to the floor. Struggling again to his feet, he got the door closed, and in a vague, misty half world of consciousness he struggled out of his clothes and got his hands on a rough towel and fumblingly dried himself.

He did not think. He was acting purely from vague instinctive realization of what he must do. He dressed again, in dry clothes, and dropped at the table. After a while he sat up and it was dark, and he knew he had blacked out again. He lighted a light and nearly dropped it to the floor. Then he stumbled to the wash basin and splashed his face with cold water. Then he bathed his scalp, feeling tenderly of the lacerations there.

A boot with a California spur. That was all he had seen. The tally book was gone, and a man wearing a new boot with a California-type spur, a large rowel, had taken it. He got coffee on, and, while he waited for it, he took his guns out and dried them painstakingly, wiping off each shell, and then replacing them in his belt with other shells from a box on a shelf.

He reloaded the guns, and then, slipping into his slicker, he went outside for his rifle. Between sips of coffee, he worked over his rifle until he was satisfied. Then he threw a small pack together and stuffed his slicker pockets with shotgun shells.

The shotgun was an express gun and short-barreled. He slung it from a loop under the slicker. Then he took a lantern and went to the stable and saddled the claybank. Leading the horse outside into the driving rain, he swung into the saddle and turned along the road toward Basin.

There was no let-up in the rain. It fell steadily and heavily, yet the claybank slogged along, alternating between a shambling trot and a fast walk. Allen Ring, his chin sunk in the upturned collar of his slicker, watched the drops fall from the brim of his Stetson and felt the bump of the shotgun under his coat.

He had seen little of the tally book, but sufficient to know that it would blow the lid off the very range war they were fearing. Knowing the Hazlitts, he knew they would bring fire and gun play to every home even remotely connected with the death of their brother.

The horse slid down a steep bank and shambled across the wide wash. Suddenly the distant roar that had been in his ears for some time sprang into consciousness and he jerked his head up. His horse snorted in alarm, and Ring stared, open-mouthed, at the wall of water, towering all of ten feet high, that was rolling down the wash toward him.

With a shrill Rebel yell he slapped the spurs to the claybank, and the startled horse turned loose with an astounded leap and hit the ground in a dead run. There was no time to slow for the bank of the wash, and the horse went up, slipped at the very brink, and started to fall back.

Ring hit the ground with both boots and scrambled over the brink, and even as the flood roared down upon them, he heaved on the bridle and the horse cleared the edge and stood, trembling. Swearing softly, Ring kicked the mud from his boots and mounted again. Leaving the raging torrent behind him, he rode on.

Thick blackness of night and heavy clouds lay upon the town when he sloped down the main street and headed the horse toward the barn. He swung down and handed the bridle to the liveryman.

"Rub him down," he said. "I'll be back."

He started for the doors, and then stopped, staring at the three horses in neighboring stalls. The liveryman noticed his glance and looked at him.

"The Hazlitts. They come in about an hour ago, ugly as sin."

Allen Ring stood, wide-legged, staring grimly out the door. There was a coolness inside him now that he recognized. He dried his hands carefully.

"Bilton in town?" he asked.

"Sure is. Playin' cards over to the Mazatzal Saloon."

"He wear Mex spurs? Big rowels?"

The man rubbed his jaw. "I don't remember. I don't know at all. You watch out," he warned. "Folks are on the prod."

Ring stepped out into the street and slogged through the mud to the edge of the boardwalk before the darkened general store. He kicked the mud from his boots and dried his hands again, after carefully unbuttoning his slicker.

Nobody would have a second chance after this. He knew well enough that his walking into the Mazatzal would precipitate an explosion. Only he wanted to light the fuse himself, in his own way.

He stood there in the darkness alone, thinking it over. They would all be there. It would be like tossing a match into a lot of fused dynamite. He wished then that he was a better man with a gun than he was or that he had someone to side him in this, but he had always acted alone and would scarcely know how to act with anyone else.

He walked along the boardwalk with long strides, his boots making hard sounds under the steady roar of the rain. He couldn't place that spur, that boot. Yet he had to. He had to get his hands on that book.

Four horses stood, heads down in the rain, saddles covered with slickers. He looked at them and saw they were of three different brands. The window of the Mazatzal was rain wet, yet standing at one side he glanced within.

The long room was crowded and smoky. Men lined the bar, feet on the brass rail. A dozen tables were crowded with card players. Everyone seemed to have taken refuge here from the rain. Picking out the Hazlitt boys, Allen saw them gathered together at the back end of the room. Then he got Ross Bilton pegged. He was at a table, playing cards, facing the door. Stan Brule was at this end of the bar, and Hagen was at a table against the wall, the three of them making three points of a flat triangle whose base was the door.

It was no accident. Bilton, then, expected trouble, and he was not looking toward the Hazlitts. Yet, on reflection, Ring could see the triangle could center fire from three directions on the Hazlitts as well. There was a man with his back to the door who sat in the game with Bilton. And not far from Hagen, Rolly Truman was at the bar.

Truman was toying with his drink, just killing time. Everybody seemed to be waiting for something. Could it be he they waited upon? No, that was scarcely to be considered. They could not know he had found the book, although it was certain at least one man in the room knew, and possibly others. Maybe it was just the tension, the building up of feeling over his taking over of the place at Red Rock. Allen Ring carefully turned down the collar of his slicker and wiped his hands dry again.

He felt jumpy and could feel that dryness in his mouth that always came on him at times like this. He touched his gun butts and then stepped over and opened the door.

Everyone looked up or around at once. Ross Bilton held a card aloft, and his hand froze at the act of dealing, holding still for a full ten seconds while Ring closed the door. He surveyed the room again and saw Ross play the card and say something in an undertone to the man opposite him. The man turned his head slightly, and it was Ben Taylor!

The gambler looked around, his face coldly curious, and for an instant their eyes met across the room, and then Allen Ring started toward him.

There was no other sound in the room, although they could all hear the unceasing roar of the rain of the roof. Ring saw something leap up in Taylor's eyes, and his own took on a sardonic glint.

"That was a good hand you dealt me down Texas way," Ring said. "A good hand!"

"You'd better draw more cards," Taylor said. "You're holdin' a small pair."

Ring's eyes shifted as the man turned slightly. It was the jingle of his spurs that drew his eyes, and there they were, the large rowelled California-style spurs, not common here. He stopped beside Taylor so the man had to tilt his head back to look up. Ring was acutely conscious that he was now centered between the fire of Brule and Hagen. The Hazlitts looked on curiously, uncertain as to what was happening.

"Give it to me, Taylor," Ring said quietly. "Give it to me now."

There was ice in his voice, and Taylor, aware of the awkwardness of his position, got to his feet, inches away from Ring.

"I don't know what you're talking about," he flared.

"No?"

Ring was standing with his feet apart a little, and his hands were breast high, one of them clutching the edge of his raincoat. He hooked with his left from that position, and the blow was too short, too sudden, and too fast for Ben Taylor.

The crack of it on the angle of his jaw was audible, and then Ring's right came up in the gambler's solar plexus and the man's knees sagged. Spinning him around, Ring ripped open his coat with a jerk that scattered buttons across the room. Then from an inside pocket he jerked the tally book.

He saw the Hazlitts start at the same instant that Bilton sprang back from the chair, upsetting it.

"Get him!" Bilton roared. "Get him!"

Ring shoved Taylor hard into the table, upsetting it and causing Bilton to spring back to keep his balance, and at the same instant Ring dropped to a half crouch and, turning left, he drew with a flash of speed and saw Brule's gun come up at almost the same instant, and then he fired!

Stan Brule was caught with his gun just level, and the bullet smashed him on the jaw. The tall man staggered, his face a mask of hatred and astonishment mingled, and then Ring fired again, doing a quick spring around with his knees bent, turning completely around in one leap, and firing as his feet hit the floor. He felt Hagen's bullet smash into him, and he tottered. Then he fired coolly, and, swinging as he fired, he caught Bilton right over the belt buckle.

It was fast action, snapping, quick, yet deliberate. The four fired shots had taken less than three seconds.

Stepping back, he scooped the tally book from the floor where it had dropped and then pocketed it. Bilton was on the floor, coughing blood. Hagen had a broken right arm and was swearing in a thick, stunned voice. Stan Brule had drawn his last gun. He had been dead before he hit the floor.

The Hazlitts started forward with a lunge, and Allen Ring took another step backward, dropping his pistol and swinging the shotgun, still hanging from his shoulder, into firing position.

"Get back!" he said thickly. "Get back or I'll kill the three of you! Back . . . back to where you stood!"

Their faces wolfish, the three stood, lean and dangerous, yet the shotgun brooked no refusal, and slowly, bitterly, and reluctantly the three moved back, step by step.

Ring motioned with the shotgun. "All of you . . . along the wall!"

The men rose and moved back, their eyes on him, uncertain, wary, some of them frightened.

Allen Ring watched them go, feeling curiously light-headed and uncertain. He tried to frown away the pain from his throbbing skull, yet there was a pervading weakness from somewhere else.

"My gosh!" Rolly Truman said. "The man's been shot! He's bleeding!"

"Get back!" Ring said thickly.

His eyes shifted to the glowing potbellied stove, and he moved forward, the shotgun waist high, his eyes on the men who stared at him, awed.

The sling held the gun level, his hand partly supporting it, a finger on the trigger. With his left hand he opened the stove and then fumbled in his pocket.

Buck Hazlitt's eyes bulged. "No!" he roared. "No, you don't!"

He lunged forward, and Ring tipped the shotgun and fired a blast into the floor, inches ahead of Hazlitt's feet. The rancher stopped so suddenly he almost fell, and the shotgun tipped to cover him.

"Back!" Ring said. He swayed on his feet. "Back!" He fished out the tally book and threw it into the flames.

Something like a sigh went through the crowd. They stared, awed as the flames seized hungrily at the opened book, curling around the leaves with hot fingers, turning them brown and then black and to ashes.

Half hypnotized the crowd watched. Then Ring's eyes swung to Hazlitt. "It was Ben Taylor killed him," he muttered. "Taylor, an' Bilton was with him. He . . . he saw it."

"We take your word for it?" Buck Hazlitt demanded furiously.

Allen Ring's eyes widened and he seemed to gather himself. "You want to question it? You want to call me a liar?"

Hazlitt looked at him, touching his tongue to his lips. "No," he said. "I figured it was them."

"I told you true," Ring said, and then his legs seemed to fold up under him and he went to the floor.

The crowd surged forward and Rolly Truman stared at Buck as Hazlitt neared the stove. The big man stared into the flames for a minute. Then he closed the door.

"Good!" he said. "Good thing! It's been a torment, that book, like a cloud hangin' over us all!"

The sun was shining through the window when Gail Truman came to see him. He was sitting up in bed and feeling better. It was good to be back on the place again, for there was much to do. She came in, slapping her boots with her quirt and smiling.

"Feel better?" she asked brightly. "You certainly look better. You've shaved."

He grinned and rubbed his jaw. "I needed it. Almost two weeks in this bed. I must have been hit bad."

"You lost a lot of blood. It's lucky you've a strong heart."

"It ain't . . . isn't so strong any more," he said. "I think it's grown mighty shaky here lately."

Gail blushed. "Oh? It has? Your nurse, I suppose?"

"She is pretty, isn't she?"

Gail looked up, alarmed. "You mean, you . . . ?"

"No, honey," he said, "you."

"Oh." She looked at him and then looked down. "Well, I guess. . . ."

"All right?"

She smiled then, suddenly and warmly. "All right."

"I had to ask you," he said. "We had to marry."

"Had to? Why?"

"People would talk, a young, lovely girl like you over at my place all the time . . . would they think you were looking at the view?"

"If they did," she replied quickly, "they'd be wrong."

"You're telling me?" he asked.

HOME IN THE VALLEY

Steve Mehan placed the folded newspaper beside his plate and watched the waiter pour his coffee. He was filled with that warm, expansive glow that comes only from a job well done, and he felt he had just cause to feel it.

Jake Hitson, the money-lending rancher from down at the end of Paiute Valley, had sneered when he heard of the attempt, and the ranchers had shaken their heads doubtfully when Steve first told them of his plan. They had agreed only because there was no alternative. He had proposed to drive a herd of cattle from the Nevada range to California in the dead of winter!

To the north the passes were blocked with snow, and to the south lay miles of trackless and almost waterless desert. Yet they had been obligated to repay the money Hitson had loaned them by the first day of March or lose their ranches to him. It had been a pitifully small amount when all was considered, yet Hitson had held their notes, and he had intended to have their range.

Months before, returning to Nevada, Steve Mehan had scouted the route. The gold rush was in full swing, people were crowding into California, and there was a demand for beef. As a boy he had packed and freighted over most of the trails and knew them well, so finally the ranchers had given in.

The drive had been a success. With surprisingly few losses he had driven the herd into central California and had sold out, a few head here and a few there, and the prices had been good.

The five ranchers of Paiute Valley who had trusted their cattle to him were safe. $25,000 in $50 gold slugs had been placed on deposit in Dake & Company's bank here in Sacramento City.

With a smile, he lifted his coffee cup. Then, as a shadow darkened his table, he glanced up to see Jake Hitson.

The man dropped into a chair opposite him, and there was a triumphant light in his eyes that made Steve suddenly wary. Yet with the gold in the bank there was nothing to make him apprehensive.

"Well, you think you've done it, don't you?" Hitson's voice was malicious. "You think you've stopped me? You've played the hero in front of Betty Bruce, and the ranchers will welcome you back with open arms. You think when everything was lost you stepped in and saved the day?"

Mehan shrugged. "We've got the money to pay you, Jake. The five brands of the Paiute will go on. This year looks like a good one, and we can drive more cattle over the route I took this time, so they'll make it now. And that in spite of all the bad years and the rustling of your friends."

Hitson chuckled. He was a big man with straw-colored brows and a flat red face. From one small spread down there at the end of the Paiute he had expanded to take in a fair portion of the valley. The methods he had used would not bear examination, and strange cattle had continued to flow into the valley, enlarging his herds. Many of the brands were open to question. The hard years and losses due to cold or drought did not affect him, because he kept adding to his herds from other sources.

During the bad years he had loaned money, and his money had been the only help available. The fact that he was a man disliked for his arrogant manner and his crooked connections made the matter only the more serious.

Hitson grinned with malice. "Read your paper yet, Mehan? If you want to spoil your breakfast, turn to page three."

Steve Mehan's dark eyes held the small blue ones of Hitson, and he felt something sick and empty in his stomach. Only bad news for him could give Hitson the satisfaction he was so obviously feeling.

Yet, even as Steve opened the paper, a man bent over the table next to him.

"Heard the news?" he asked excitedly. "Latch and Evans banking house has failed. That means that Dake and Company are gone, too. They'll close the doors. There's already a line out there a hundred yards long and still growin'!"

Steve opened his paper slowly. The news was there for all to read. Latch & Evans had failed. The managing director had flown the coop, and only one interpretation could be put upon that. Dake & Company, always closely associated with Latch & Evans, would be caught in the collapse. February of 1855 would see the end of the five brands of Paiute Valley. It would be the end of everything he had planned, everything he wanted for Betty.

"See?" Hitson sneered, heaving himself to his feet. "Try and play hero now. I've got you and them highfalutin' friends of yours where I want 'em. I'll kick every cussed one of 'em into the trail on March First, and with pleasure. And that goes for you, Steve Mehan."

Steve scarcely heard him. He was remembering that awful drive. The hard winds, the bitter cold, the bawling cattle. And then the desert, the Indians, the struggle to get through with the herd intact—and all to end in this. Collapse and failure. Yes, and the lives of two men had been sacrificed, the two who had been killed on the way over the trail.

Mehan remembered Chuck Farthing's words.

He had gone down with a Mojave Indian's bullet in his chest.

"Get 'em through, boy. Save the old man's ranch for him. That's all I ask."

It had been little enough for two lives. And now they were gone, for nothing.

The realization hit Steve Mehan like a blow and brought him to his feet fighting mad, his eyes blazing, his jaw set.

"I'll be eternally blasted if they have!" he exploded, although only he knew what he meant.

He started for the door, leaving his breakfast unfinished behind him, his mind working like lightning. The whole California picture lay open for him now. The news of the failure would have reached the Dake & Company branches in Marysville and Grass Valley. And in Placerville. There was no hope there.

Portland? He stopped short, his eyes narrowed with thought. Didn't they have a branch in Portland? Of course! He remembered it well, now that he thought of it. The steamer from San Francisco would leave the next morning, and it would be carrying the news. But what if he could beat that steamer to Portland?

Going by steamer himself would be futile, for he would arrive at the same time the news did, and there would be no chance for him to get his money. Hurrying down the street, his eyes scanning the crowds for Pink Egan and Jerry

Smith, cowpunchers who had made the drive with him, he searched out every possible chance, and all that remained was that seven hundred miles of trail between Sacramento and Portland, rough, and part of it harassed by warring Modocs.

He paused, glancing around. He was a tall young man with rusty brown hair and a narrow, rather scholarly face. To the casual observer he looked like a roughly dressed frontier doctor or lawyer. Actually he was a man bred to the saddle and the wild country.

Over the roofs of the buildings he could see the smoke of a steamboat. It was the stern-wheeler *Belle*, just about to leave for Knights Landing, forty-two miles upstream.

He started for the gangway, walking fast, and, just as he reached it, a hand caught his sleeve. He wheeled to see Pink and Jerry at his elbow.

"Hey!" Smith demanded. "Where you goin' so fast?"

"We run two blocks to catch up with you."

Quickly Steve explained. The riverboat tooted its whistle, and the crew started for the gangway to haul it aboard. "It's our only chance!" Steve Mehan exclaimed. "I've got to beat that steamboat from Frisco to Portland and draw my money before they get the news. Don't tell anybody where I've gone, and keep your eyes on Hitson."

He lunged for the gangway and raced aboard. It was foolish, it was wild, it was impossible, but it was their only chance. Grimly he recalled what he had told Betty Bruce when he left the valley. "I'll get them cattle over, honey, or I'll die trying."

"You come back, Steve," she had begged. "That's all I ask. We can always go somewhere and start over. We always have each other."

"I know, honey, but how about your father? How about Pete Farthing? They're too old to start over, and the ranches are all they have. They worked like slaves, fought Indians, gave a lot in sweat and blood for their ranches. I'll not see 'em turned out now. Whatever comes, I'll make it."

As the riverboat pushed away from the dock, he glanced back. Jake Hitson was staring after him, his brow furrowed. Jake had seen him, and that was bad.

Mehan put such thoughts behind him. The boat would not take long to get to Knights Landing, and he could depend upon Knight to help him. The man had migrated from New Mexico fifteen years before, but he had known Steve's father, and they had come over the Santa Fe Trail together. From a mud-and-wattle hut on an Indian mound at the landing, he had built a land grant he got from his Mexican wife into a fine estate, and the town had been named for him.

Would Jake Hitson guess what he was attempting? If so, what could he do? The man had money, and with money one can do many things. Hitson would not stop at killing. Steve had more than a hunch that Hitson had urged the Mojaves into the attack on the cattle drive that had resulted in the death of Chuck Farthing. He had more than a hunch that the landslide that had killed Dixie Rollins had been due to more than purely natural causes. But he could prove nothing.

His only chance was to reach Portland before the news did. He was not worried about their willingness to pay him the money. The banks made a charge of one half of one percent for all withdrawals over $1,000, and it would look like easy profit to the agent at the banking and express house.

Nor was it all unfamiliar country, for Steve had spent two years punching cows on ranches, prospecting and hunting through the northern valleys, almost as far as the Oregon line.

When the *Belle* shouldered her comfortable bulk against the landing at Knights, Mehan did not wait for the gangway. He grabbed the bulwark and vaulted ashore, landing on his hands and knees.

He found Knight standing on the steps of his home, looking down toward the river.

"A hoss, Steve?" Knight repeated. "Shorest thing you know. What's up?"

While Steve threw a saddle on a tall chestnut, he explained briefly.

"You'll never make it, boy," Knight protested. "It's a hard drive, and the Modocs are raidin' again." He chewed on his mustache as Steve swung into the saddle. "Boy," he said, "when you get to the head of Grand Island, see the judge. He's an old friend of mine, and he'll let you have a hoss. Good luck."

Steve wheeled the chestnut into the street and started north at a spanking trot. He kept the horse moving, and the long-legged chestnut had a liking for the trail. He moved out eagerly, seeming to catch some of the anxiety to get over the trail that filled his rider.

At the head of Grand Island, Steve swapped horses and started north again, holding grimly to the trail. There was going to be little time for rest and less time to eat. He would have to keep moving if he was going to make it. The trail over much of the country was bad, and the farther north he got toward the line, the worse it would be.

His friends on the ranches remembered him, and he repeatedly swapped horses and kept moving. The sun was setting in a rose of glory when he made his fourth change of mount near the Marysville Buttes. The purple haze of evening was gathering when he turned up the trail and lined out.

He had money with him, and he paid a bonus plus a blown horse when necessary. But the stockmen were natural allies, as were the freighters along the route, and they were always willing to help. After leaving Knights Landing he had told no one his true mission, his only explanation being that he was after a thief. In a certain sense, that was exactly true.

At 10:00 p.m., ten hours out of Sacramento, he galloped into the dark streets of Red Bluffs. No more than five minutes later, clutching a sandwich in his hand and with a fresh horse under him, he was off again.

Darkness closed around him, and the air was cool. He had no rifle with him, only the pistol he habitually wore and plenty of ammunition.

The air was so cold that he drew his coat around him, tucking it under and around his legs. He spoke softly to the horse, and its ears twitched. It was funny about a horse—how much they would give for gentleness. There was no animal that responded so readily to good treatment, and no other animal would run itself to death for a man—except, occasionally, a dog.

The hoofs of the horse beat a pounding rhythm upon the trail, and Steve leaned forward in the saddle, hunching himself against the damp chill and to cut wind resistance. His eyes were alert, although weariness began to dull his muscles and take the drive and snap from them.

Twenty miles out of Red Bluffs he glimpsed a fire shining through the trees. He slowed the horse, putting a hand on its damp neck. It was a campfire. He could see the light reflecting from the front of a covered wagon, and he heard voices speaking. He rode nearer and saw the faces of the men come around toward him.

"Who's there?" A tall man stepped around the fire with a rifle in his hand.

"Mehan, a cattleman. I'm after a thief and need a fresh horse."

"Well, light and talk. You won't catch him on that hoss. Damn' fine animal," he added, "but you've shore put him over the road."

"He's got heart, that one!" Steve said, slapping the horse. "Plenty of it. Is that coffee I smell?"

The bearded man picked up the pot. "It shore is, pardner. Have some." He poured a cupful, handed it to Steve, and then strolled over to the horse. "Shucks, with a rub-down and a blanket he'll be all right. Tell you what I'll do. I've got a buckskin here that'll run till he drops. Give me twenty to boot and he's yours."

Mehan looked up. "Done, but you throw in a couple of sandwiches."

The bearded man chuckled. "Shore will." He glanced at the saddle as Steve began stripping it from the horse. "You've got no rifle?"

"No, only a pistol. I'll take my chances."

"Haven't got a rifle to spare, but I'll make you

a deal on this." He handed Steve a four-barreled Braendlin repeating pistol. "Frankly, mister, I need money. Got my family down to Red Bluffs, and I don't want to come in broke."

"How much?"

"Another twenty?"

"Sure, if you've got ammunition for it."

"I've got a hundred rounds. And it goes with the gun." The man dug out the ammunition. "Joe, wrap up a couple of them sandwiches for the man. Got smokin'?"

"Sure thing." Steve swung into the saddle and pocketed the extra pistol. He put the ammunition in his saddlebags. "Good luck."

"Hope you catch him!" the man called.

Steve touched a spur lightly to the big buckskin and was gone in a clatter of hoofs. Behind him the fire twinkled lonesomely among the dark columns of the trees, and then as he went down beyond a rise, the light faded, and he was alone in the darkness, hitting the road at a fast trot.

Later, he saw the white radiance that preceded the moon, and something else—the white, gleaming peak of Mount Shasta, one of the most beautiful mountains in the world. Lifting its fourteen-thousand-foot peak above the surrounding country, it was like a throne for the Great Spirit of the Indians.

In darkness and moving fast, Steve Mehan rode

down the trail into Shasta and then on to Whiskeytown.

A drunken miner lurched from the side of a building and flagged him down. "No use hurryin'," he said. "It ain't true!"

"What ain't true?" Steve stared at him. "What you talking about?"

"That Whiskey Creek. Shucks, it's got water in it just like any creek." He spat with disgust. "I come all the way down here from Yreka huntin' it."

"You came from Yreka?" Steve grabbed his shoulder. "How's the trail? Any Indians out?"

"Trail?" The miner spat. "There ain't no trail! A loose-minded mule walked through the brush a couple of times, that's all. Indians? Modocs? Man, the woods is full of 'em! Behind ever' bush! Scalp-huntin' bucks, young and old. If you're headin' that way, you won't get through. Your hair will be in a teepee 'fore two suns go down."

He staggered off into the darkness, trying a song that dribbled away and lost itself in the noise of the creek.

Mehan walked the horse down to the creek and let him drink.

"No whiskey, but we'll settle for water, won't we, Buck?"

The creek had its name, he remembered, from an ornery mule that lost the barrel from its pack.

It broke in Whiskey Creek, which promptly drew a name upon itself.

Steve Mehan started the horse again, heading for the stage station at Tower House, some ten miles up the road. The buckskin was weary but game. Ahead of him and on his right still loomed the peak of Mount Shasta, seeming large in the occasional glimpses, even at the distance that still separated them.

He almost fell from his horse at Tower House, with dawn bright in the eastern sky beyond the ragged mountains. The stage tender blinked sleepy eyes at him and then at the horse.

"You've been givin' her blazes," he said. "In a mite of hurry?"

"After a thief," mumbled Steve.

The man scratched his grizzled chin. "He must be a goin' son-of-a-gun," he commented whimsically. "Want anything?"

"Breakfast and a fresh horse."

"Easy done. You ain't figurin' on ridin' north, are you? Better change your plans if you are, because the Modocs are out and they're in a killin' mood. No trail north of here, you know."

With a quick breakfast and what must have been a gallon of coffee under his belt, Steve Mehan swung into the saddle and started once more. The new horse was a gray and built for the trail. Steve was sodden with weariness, and at every moment his lids fluttered and started to close. But now, for a while at least, he dared not close them.

Across Clear Creek he rode into the uplands where no wagon road had ever been started. It was a rugged country, but one he remembered from the past, and he weaved around among the trees, following the thread of what might have been a trail. Into a labyrinth of cañons he rode, following the vague trail up the bottom of a gorge, now in the water, then out of it. Then he climbed a steep trail out of the gorge and headed out across the long rolling swell of a grass-covered mountainside.

The air was much colder now, and there was an occasional flurry of snow. At times he clung to the saddle horn, letting the horse find his own trail, just so that trail was north. He rode into the heavily forested sides of the Trinity Mountains, losing the trail once in the dimness under the tall firs and tamaracks, but keeping on his northern route. Eventually he again hit what must have been the trail.

His body ached, and he fought to keep his eyelids open. Once he dismounted and walked for several miles to keep himself awake and to give the horse a slight rest. Then he was back in the saddle and riding once more.

Behind him somewhere was Jake Hitson. Jake, he knew well, would not give up easily. If he guessed what Mehan was attempting, he would stop at nothing to prevent it. And yet there was no way of preventing it unless he came north with the boat and reached Portland before him. And that would do no good, for if the boat got to Portland before him, the news would be there, and nothing Hitson could do would be any worse than the arrival of that news.

Egan and Smith would have their eyes on Jake Hitson, but he might find some means of getting away. Certainly, Steve thought grimly, nothing on horseback was going to catch him now.

The wind grew still colder and howled mournfully under the dark, needled trees. He shivered and hunched his shoulders against the wind. Once, half asleep, he almost fell from the horse when the gray shied at a fleeing rabbit.

As yet there were no Indians. He peered ahead across the bleak and forbidding countryside, but it was empty. And then, not long later, he turned down a well-marked trail to Trinity Creek.

He swung down in front of a log bunkhouse. A miner was at the door.

"A hoss?" The miner chuckled. "Stranger, you're shore out of luck. There ain't a hoss hereabouts you could get for love or money."

Steve Mehan sagged against the building. "Mister," he mumbled, "I've just got to get a horse. I've got to."

"Sorry, son. There just ain't none. Nobody in town would give up his hoss right now, and they are mighty scarce at that. You'd better come in and have some coffee."

Steve stripped his saddle and bridle from his horse and walked into the house. He almost fell into a chair. Several miners playing cards looked up. *"Amigo,"* one of them said, "you'd better lay off that stuff."

Mehan's head came up heavily, and he peered at the speaker, a blond giant in a red-checked shirt.

"I haven't slept since I left Sacramento," he said. "Been in the saddle ever since."

"Sacramento?" The young man stared. "You must be crazy."

"He's chasin' a thief," said the miner Steve had first seen. He was bringing Steve a cup of coffee. "I'd want a man awful bad before I rode like that."

"I got to beat the steamer to Portland," Steve said. It was a lie in a way, but actually the truth. "If I don't, the fellow will get away with fifteen thousand dollars."

"Fifteen thou. . . ." The young man laid down his hand. "Brother," he said emphatically, "I'd ride, too."

Steve gulped the coffee and lurched to his feet.

"Got to find a horse," he said, and lunged outside.

It took him less than a half hour to prove to himself that it was an impossibility. Nobody would even consider selling a horse, and his own was in bad shape.

"Not a chance," they told him. "A man without a hoss in this country is through. No way in or out but on a hoss, and not an extry in town."

He walked back to the stable. One look at his own horse told him the animal was through. There was no chance to go farther with it. No matter what he might do, the poor creature could stagger no more than a few miles. It would be killing a good horse to no purpose. Disgusted and discouraged, numbed with weariness, he stood in the cold wind, rubbing his grizzled chin with a fumbling hand.

So this was the end. After all his effort, the drive over the mountains and desert, the long struggle to get back, and then this ride, and all for nothing. Back there in the Paiute the people he had left behind would be trusting him, keeping their faith. For no matter how much they were sure he would fail, their hopes must go with him. And now he had failed.

Wearily he staggered into the bunkhouse and dropped into his chair. He fumbled with the coffee pot and succeeded in pouring out a cupful. His legs and feet felt numb, and he had never realized a man could be so utterly, completely tired.

The young man in the checkered shirt looked around from his poker game.

"No luck, eh? You've come a long way to lose now."

Steve nodded bitterly. "That money belongs to my friends as well as me," he said. "That's the worst of it."

The blond young fellow laid down his hand and pulled in the chips. Then he picked up his pipe.

"My sorrel out there in the barn," he said, "is the best hoss on the Trinity. You take it and go, but man, you'd better get yourself some rest at Scott Valley. You'll die."

Mehan lunged to his feet, hope flooding the weariness from his body.

"How much?" he demanded, reaching for his pocket.

"Nothin'," the fellow said. "Only if you catch that thief, bring him back on my hoss, and I'll help you hang him. I promise you."

Steve hesitated. "What about the horse?"

"Bring him back when you come south," the fellow said, "and take care of him. He'll never let you down."

Steve Mehan rode out of Trinity Creek ten minutes later, and the sorrel took to the trail as if he knew all that was at stake, and pressed on eagerly for Scott Valley.

The cold was increasing as Steve Mehan rode farther north, and the wind was raw, spitting rain that seemed to be changing to snow. Head hunched behind the collar of his buffalo coat, Steve pushed on, talking low to the horse, whose ears twitched a response and who kept going, alternating between a fast walk and a swinging, space-eating trot.

Six hours out of Trinity Creek, Steve Mehan rode into Scott Valley.

The stage tender took one look at him and waved him to a bunk.

"Hit it, stranger," he said. "I'll care for your hoss!" Stumbling through a fog of exhaustion, Steve made the bunk and dropped into its softness. . . .

Steve Mehan opened his eyes suddenly, with the bright sunlight in his face. He glanced at his watch. It was noon.

Lunging to his feet, he pulled on his boots, which somebody had removed without awakening him, and reached for his coat. The heavy-set red-haired stage tender walked in and glanced at him.

"See you've got Joe Chalmers's hoss," he remarked, his thumbs in his belt. "How come?"

Steve looked up. "Chasing a thief. He let me have it."

"I know Chalmers. He wouldn't let Moses have this hoss to lead the Israelites out of Egypt. Not him. You've got some explainin' to do, stranger."

"I said he loaned me the horse," Steve said

grimly. "I'm leaving him with you and I want to buy another to go on with. What have you got?"

Red was dubious. "Don't reckon I should sell you one. Looks mighty funny to me, you havin' Joe's hoss. Is Joe all right?"

"Well," Steve said wearily, "he was just collecting a pot levied by three treys when I talked to him, so I reckon he'll make out."

Red chuckled. "He's a poker-playin' man, that one. Good man, too." He hesitated, and then shrugged. "All right. There's a blaze-faced black in the stable you can have for fifty dollars. Good horse, too. Better eat somethin'."

He put food on the table, and Steve ate too rapidly. He gulped some coffee, and then Red came out with a pint of whiskey.

"Stick this in your pocket, stranger. Might come in handy."

"Thanks." Mehan wiped his mouth and got to his feet. He felt better, and he walked to the door.

"You ain't got a rifle?" Red was frankly incredulous. "The Modocs will get you shore."

"Haven't seen hide nor hair of one yet," Steve said, smiling. "I'm beginning to think they've all gone East for the winter."

"Don't you think it." Red slipped a bridle on the black while Steve cinched up the saddle. "They are out, and things up Oregon way are bad off. They shore raised ructions up around Grave

Creek, and all the country around the Klamath and the Rogue is harassed by 'em."

Somewhere out at sea the steamer would be plowing over the gray sea toward Astoria and the mouth of the Columbia. The trip from there up to the Willamette and Portland would not take long.

The black left town at a fast lope and held it. The horse was good, no question about it. Beyond Callahan's, Steve hit the old Applegate wagon trail and found the going somewhat better and pushed on. Just seventy hours out from Knights Landing he rode into Yreka.

After a quick meal, a drink, and a fresh horse, he mounted and headed out of town for the Oregon line. He rode through Humbug City and Hawkinsville without a stop and followed a winding trail up the gorge of the Shasta.

Once, after climbing the long slope north of the Klamath, he glimpsed a party of Indians some distance away. They sighted him, for they turned their horses his way, but he rode on, holding his pace, and crossed Hungry Creek and left behind him the cairn that marked the boundary line of Oregon. He turned away from the trail then and headed into the back country, trying a cut-off for Bear Creek and the village of Jacksonville. Somewhere, he lost the Indians.

He pushed on, and now the rain that had been falling intermittently turned to snow. It began to fall, thick and fast. He was riding out of the trees when on the white-flecked earth before him he saw a moccasin track with earth just tumbling into it from the edge.

Instantly he whipped his horse around and touched spurs to its flanks. The startled animal gave a great bound, and at the same instant a shot whipped by where he had been only a moment before. Then he was charging through brush, and the horse was dodging among the trees.

An Indian sprang from behind a rock and lifted a rifle. Steve drew and fired. The Indian threw his rifle away and rolled over on the ground, moaning.

Wild yells chorused behind him, and a shot cut the branches overhead. He fired again and then again.

Stowing the Smith & Wesson away, he whipped out the four-barreled Braendlin. Holding it ready, he charged out of the brush and headed across the open country. Behind him the Modocs were coming fast. His horse was quick and alert, and he swung it around a grove of trees and down into a gully. Racing along the bottom, he hit a small stream and began walking the horse carefully upstream. After making a half mile, he rode out again and took to the timber, reloading his other pistol.

Swapping horses at every chance, he pushed on. One hundred and forty-three hours out of Knights Landing, he rode into Portland. He had covered six hundred and fifty-five miles. He swung down and turned to the stable hand.

"That steamer in from Frisco?"

"Heard her whistle," said the man. "She's comin' up the river now."

But Steve had turned and was running fast.

The agent for the banking express company looked up and blinked when Steve Mehan lurched through the door.

"I'm buying cattle," Steve told him, "and need some money. Can you honor a certificate of deposit for me?"

"Let's see her."

Steve handed him the order and shifted restlessly. The man eyed the order for a long time, and then turned it over and studied the back. Finally, when Steve was almost beside himself with impatience, the agent looked up over his glasses at the bearded, hollow-eyed young man. "Reckon I can," he said. "Of course there's the deduction of one half of one percent for all amounts over a thousand dollars."

"Pay me," Steve said.

He leaned over the desk, and suddenly the deep-toned blast of the steamer's whistle rang through the room. The agent was putting stacks of gold on the table. He looked up.

"Well, what do you know? That's the steamer in. I reckon I better see about. . . ."

Whatever he was going to see about, Steve

never discovered, for as the agent turned away, Steve reached out and collared him. "Pay me," he said sharply. "Pay me now."

The agent shrugged. "Well, all right. No need to get all fussed about it. Plenty of time."

He put out stacks of gold. Mentally Steve calculated the amount. When it was all there, he swept it into a sack—almost fifty pounds of gold. He slung the sack over his shoulder and turned toward the door.

A gun boomed, announcing the arrival of the steamer, as he stepped out into the street. Four men were racing up the street from the dock, and the man in the lead was Jake Hitson.

Hitson skidded to a halt when he saw Steve Mehan, and his face went dark with angry blood. The blue eyes frosted and he stood wide-legged, staring at the man who had beaten him to Portland.

"So!" His voice was a roar that turned the startled townspeople around. "Beat me here, did you? Got your money, have you?" He seemed unable to absorb the fact that he was beaten, that Mehan had made it through.

"Just so you won't kick anybody out of his home, Jake," Steve said quietly, "and I hope that don't hurt too much."

The small man in the black suit had gone around them and into the express company office. The other men were Pink Egan and a swarthy-faced man who was obviously a friend of Hitson's.

Hitson lowered his head. The fury seemed to go out of him as he stood there in the street with a soft rain falling over them.

"You won't get back there," he said in a dead, flat voice. "You done it, all right, but you'll never play the hero in Paiute, because I'm goin' to kill you."

"Like you killed Dixie and Chuck?" challenged Steve. "You did, you know. You started that landslide and the Mojaves."

Hitson made no reply. He merely stood there, a huge bull of a man, his frosty eyes bright and hard under the corn-silk eyebrows.

Suddenly his hand swept down.

When Steve had first sighted the man, he had lowered the sack of gold to the street. Now he swept his coat back and grabbed for his own gun. He was no gunfighter, and the glimpse of flashing speed from Hitson made something go sick within him, but his gun came up and he fired.

Hitson's gun was already flaming, and even as Steve pulled the trigger on his own gun, a bullet from Hitson's pistol knocked the Smith & Wesson spinning into the dust! Steve sprang back and heard the hard, dry laugh of triumph from Jake Hitson's throat.

"Now I'll kill you!" Hitson yelled.

The killer's eyes were cold as he lifted the pistol, but, even as it came level, Steve hurled himself to his knees and jerked out the four-barreled Braendlin.

Hitson swung the gun down on him, but, startled by Steve's movement, he swung too fast and shot too fast. The bullet ripped through the top of Mehan's shoulder, tugging hard at the heavy coat. Then Steve fired. He fired once, twice, three times, and then heaved himself erect and stepped to one side, holding his last shot ready, his eyes careful.

Hitson stood stockstill, his eyes puzzled. Blood was trickling from his throat, and there was a slowly spreading blot of blood on his white shirt. He tried to speak, but when he opened his mouth, blood frothed there, and he started to back up, frowning.

He stumbled and fell. Slowly he rolled over on his face in the street. Blood turned the gravel crimson, and rain darkened the coat on his back.

Only then did Steve Mehan look up. Pink Egan, his face cold, had a gun leveled at Hitson's companion. "You beat it," Pink said. "You get goin'!"

"Shore." The man backed away, staring at Hitson's body. "Shore, I'm gone. I don't want no trouble. I just come along, I. . . ."

The small man in black came out of the express office.

"Got here just in time," he said. "I'm the purser from the steamer. Got nearly a thousand out of that bank, the last anybody will get." He smiled at Mehan. "Won another thousand on your ride. I bet on you and got two to one." He chuckled. "Of course, I knew we had soldiers to put ashore at two places coming north, and that helped. I'm a sporting man, myself." He clinked the gold in his sack and smiled, twitching his mustache with a white finger. "Up to a point," he added, smiling again. "Only up to a point."

WEST IS WHERE THE HEART IS

Jim London lay face down in the dry prairie grass, his body pressed tightly against the ground. Heat, starvation, and exhaustion had taken a toll of his lean, powerful body, and, although light-headed from their accumulative effects, he still grasped the fact that to survive he must not be seen.

Hot sun blazed upon his back, and in his nostrils was the stale, sour smell of clothes and body long unwashed. Behind him lay days of dodging Comanche war parties and sleeping on the bare ground behind rocks or under bushes. He was without weapons or food, and it had been nine hours since he had tasted water, and that was only dew he had licked from leaves.

The screams of the dying rang in his ears, amid the sounds of occasional shots and the shouts and war cries of the Indians. From a hill almost five miles away he had spotted the white canvas tops of the Conestoga wagons and had taken a course that would intercept them. And then, in the last few minutes before he could reach their help, the Comanches had hit the wagon train.

From the way the attack went, a number of the Indians must have been bedded down in the tall grass, keeping out of sight, and then, when the train was passing, they sprang for the drivers of the teams. The strategy was perfect, for there was then no chance of the wagon train making its circle. The lead wagons did swing, but two other teamsters were dead and another was fighting for his life, and their wagons could not be turned. The two lead wagons found themselves isolated from the last four and were hit hard by at least twenty Indians. The wagon whose driver was fighting turned over in the tall grass at the edge of a ditch, and the driver was killed.

Within twenty minutes after the beginning of the attack, the fighting was over and the wagons looted, and the Indians were riding away, leaving behind them only dead and butchered oxen, the scalped and mutilated bodies of the drivers, and the women who were killed or who had killed themselves.

Yet Jim London did not move. This was not his first crossing of the plains or his first encounter with Indians. He had fought Comanches before, as well as Kiowas, Apaches, Sioux, and Cheyennes. Born on the Oregon Trail, he had later been a teamster on the Santa Fe. He knew better than to move now. He knew that an Indian or two might come back to look for more loot.

The smoke of the burning wagons bit at his

nostrils, yet he waited. An hour had passed before he let himself move, and then it was only to inch to the top of the hill, where from behind a tuft of bunch grass he surveyed the scene before him.

No living thing stirred near the wagons. Slow tendrils of smoke lifted from blackened timbers and wheel spokes. Bodies lay scattered about, grotesque in attitudes of tortured death. For a long time he studied the scene below, and the surrounding hills. And then he crawled over the skyline and slithered downhill through the grass, making no more visible disturbance than a snake or a coyote.

This was not the first such wagon train he had come upon, and he knew there was every chance that he would find food among the ruins as well as water, perhaps even overlooked weapons. Indians looted hastily and took the more obvious things, usually scattering food and wasting what they could not easily carry away.

Home was still more than two hundred miles away, and the wife he had not seen in four years would be waiting for him. In his heart, he knew she would be waiting. During the war the others had scoffed at him.

"Why, Jim, you say yourself she don't even know where you're at. She probably figures you're dead. No woman can be expected to wait that long. Not for a man she never hears of and when she's in a good country for men and a bad one for women."

"She'll wait. I know Jane."

"No man knows a woman that well. No man could. You say yourself you come East with a wagon train in 'Sixty-One. Now it's 'Sixty-Four. You been in the war, you been wounded, you ain't been home, nor heard from her, nor she from you. Worst of all, she was left on a piece of ground with only a cabin built, no ground broke, no close up neighbors. I'll tell you, Jim, you're crazy. Come, go to Mexico with us."

"No," he had said stubbornly. "I'll go home. I'll go back to Jane. I came East after some fixings for her, after some stock for the ranch, and I'll go home with what I set out after."

"You got any young 'uns?" The big sergeant had been skeptical.

"Nope. I sure ain't, but I wish I did. Only," he had added, "maybe I have. Jane, she was expecting, but had a time to go when I left. I only figured to be gone four months."

"And you been gone four years?" The sergeant had shook his head. "Forget her, Jim, and come with us. Nobody would deny she was a good woman. From what you tell of her, she sure was, but she's been alone and no doubt figures you're dead. She'll be married again, maybe with a family."

Jim London had shaken his head. "I never took

up with no other woman, and Jane wouldn't take up with any other man. I'm going home."

He had made a good start. He had saved nearly every dime of pay, and he did some shrewd buying and trading when the war was over. He started West with a small but good train, and he had two wagons with six head of mules to the wagon, knowing the mules would sell better in New Mexico than would oxen. He had six cows and a yearling bull, some pigs, chickens, and utensils. He was a proud man when he looked over his outfit, and he hired two boys with the train to help him with the extra wagon and the stock.

Comanches hit them before they were well started. They killed two men, and one woman and stampeded some stock. The wagon train continued, and at the forks of Little Creek they struck again, in force this time, and only Jim London came out of it alive. All his outfit was gone, and he escaped without weapons, food, or water.

He lay flat in the grass at the edge of the burned spot. Again he studied the hills, and then he eased forward and got to his feet. The nearest wagon was upright, and smoke was still rising from it. The wheels were partly burned, the box badly charred, and the interior smoking. It was still too hot to touch.

He crouched near the front wheel and studied

the situation, avoiding the bodies. No weapons were in sight, but he had scarcely expected any. There had been nine wagons. The lead wagons were thirty or forty yards off, and the three wagons whose drivers had been attacked were bunched in the middle with one overturned. The last four, near one of which he was crouched, had burned further than the others.

Suddenly he saw a dead horse lying at one side with a canteen tied to the saddle. He crossed to it at once, and, tearing the canteen loose, he rinsed his mouth with water. Gripping himself tight against drinking, he rinsed his mouth again and moistened his cracked lips. Only then did he let a mere swallow trickle down his parched throat.

Resolutely he put the canteen down in the shade and went through the saddle pockets. It was a treasure trove. He found a good-size chunk of almost iron-hard brown sugar, a half dozen biscuits, a chunk of jerky wrapped in paper, and a new plug of chewing tobacco. Putting these things with the canteen, he unfastened the slicker from behind the saddle and added that to the pile.

Wagon by wagon he searched, always alert to the surrounding country and at times leaving the wagons to observe the plain from a hilltop. It was quite dark before he was finished. Then he took his first good drink, for he had allowed himself only nips during the remainder of the day. He took his drink, and then ate a biscuit, and chewed a piece of the jerky. With his hunting knife he shaved a little of the plug tobacco and made a cigarette by rolling it in paper, the way the Mexicans did.

Every instinct warned him to be away from the place by daylight, and, as much as he disliked leaving the bodies as they were, he knew it would be folly to bury them. If the Indians passed that way again, they would find them buried and would immediately be on his trail.

Crawling along the edge of the taller grass near the depression where the wagon had tipped over, he stopped suddenly. Here in the ground near the edge of the grass was a boot print!

His fingers found it, and then felt carefully. It had been made by a running man, either large or heavily laden. Feeling his way along the tracks, London stopped again, for this time his hand had come in contact with a boot. He shook it, but there was no move or response. Crawling nearer he touched the man's hand. It was cold as marble in the damp night air.

Moving his hand again, he struck canvas. Feeling along it he found it was a long canvas sack. Evidently the dead man had grabbed this sack from the wagon and dashed for the shelter of the ditch or hollow. Apparently he had been struck by a bullet and killed, but, feeling again of the body, London's hand came in contact with a belt gun. So the Comanches had not found him!

Stripping the belt and gun from the dead man, London swung it around his own hips, and then checked the gun. It was fully loaded, and so were the cartridge loops in the belt.

Something stirred in the grass, and instantly he froze, sliding out his hunting knife. He waited for several minutes, and then he heard it again. Something alive lay here in the grass with him!

A Comanche? No Indian likes to fight at night, and he had seen no Indians anywhere near when darkness fell. No, if anything lived near him now, it must be something, man or animal, from the wagon train. For a long time he lay still, thinking it over, and then he took a chance. Yet from his experience the chance was not a long one.

"If there is someone there, speak up."

There was no sound, and he waited, listening. Five minutes passed—ten—twenty. Carefully, then, he slid through the grass, changing his position, and then froze in place. Something was moving, quite near!

His hand shot out, and he was shocked to find himself grasping a small hand with a ruffle of cloth at the wrist! The child struggled violently, and he whispered hoarsely: "Be still. I'm a friend. If you run, the Indians might come." Instantly the struggling stopped. "There," he breathed. "That's better." He searched his mind for something reassuring to say, and finally said: "Damp here, isn't it? Don't you have a coat?"

There was a momentary silence, and then a small voice said: "It was in the wagon."

"We'll look for it pretty soon," London said. "My name's Jim. What's yours?"

"Betty Jane Jones. I'm five years old and my papa's name is Daniel Jones and he is forty-six. Are you forty-six?"

London grinned. "No, I'm just twenty-nine, Betty Jane." He hesitated a minute, and then said: "Betty Jane, you strike me as a mighty brave little girl. There when I first heard you, you made no more noise than a rabbit. Now do you think you can keep that up?"

"Yes." It was a very small voice but it sounded sure.

"Good. Now listen, Betty Jane." Quietly he told her where he had come from and where he was going. He did not mention her parents, and she did not ask about them. From that he decided she knew only too well what had happened to them and the others from the wagon train.

"There's a canvas sack here, and I've got to look into it. Maybe there's something we can use. We're going to need food, Betty Jane, and a rifle. Later, we're going to have to find horses and money."

The sound of his voice, low though it was, seemed to give her confidence. She crawled nearer to him, and, when she felt the sack, she

161

said: "That's Daddy's bag. He keeps his carbine in it and his best clothes."

"Carbine?" London fumbled open the sack.

"Is a carbine like a rifle?"

He told her it was, and then found the gun. It was carefully wrapped, and by the feel of it London could tell the weapon was new or almost new. There was ammunition, another pistol, and a small canvas sack that chinked softly with gold coins. He stuffed this in his pocket. A careful check of the remaining wagons netted him nothing more, but he was not disturbed. The guns he had were good ones, and he had a little food and the canteen. Gravely he took Betty Jane's hand and they started.

They walked for an hour before her steps began to drag, and then he picked her up and carried her. By the time the sky had grown gray, he figured they had come six or seven miles from the burned wagons. He found some solid ground among some reeds on the edge of a slough, and they settled down there for the day.

After making coffee with a handful found in one of the only partly burned wagons, London gave Betty Jane some of the jerky and a biscuit. Then for the first time he examined his carbine. His eyes brightened as he sized it up. It was a Ball & Lamson Repeating Carbine, a gun just on the market and of which this must have been one of the first sold. It was a seven-shot weapon carrying a .56-50 cartridge. It was almost thirty-eight inches in length and weighed a bit over seven pounds.

The pistols were also new, both Prescott Navy six-shooters, caliber .38 with rosewood grips. Betty Jane looked at them and tears welled into her eyes. He took her hand quickly.

"Don't cry, honey. Your dad would want me to use the guns to take care of his girl. You've been mighty brave. Now keep it up."

She looked up at him with woebegone eyes, but the tears stopped, and after a while she fell asleep.

There was little shade, and, as the reeds were not tall, he did not dare stand up. They kept close to the edge of the reeds and lay perfectly still. Once he heard a horse walking not far away and heard low, guttural voices and a hacking cough. He caught only a fleeting glimpse of one rider and hoped the Indians would not find their tracks.

When night came, they started on once more. He took his direction by the stars and he walked steadily, carrying Betty Jane most of the distance. Sometimes when she walked beside him, she talked. She rambled on endlessly about her home, her dolls, and her parents. Then on the third day she mentioned Hurlburt.

"He was a bad man. My papa told Mama he

was a bad man. Papa said he was after Mister Ballard's money."

"Who was Hurlburt?" London asked, more to keep the child occupied than because he wanted to know.

"He tried to steal Daddy's new carbine, and Mister Ballard said he was a thief. He told him so."

Hurlburt. The child might be mispronouncing the name, but it sounded like that. There had been a man in Independence by that name. He had not been liked—a big, bearded man, very quarrelsome.

"Did he have a beard, Betty Jane? A big, black beard?"

She nodded eagerly. "At first, he did. But he didn't have it when he came back with the Indians."

"What?" He turned so sharply toward her that her eyes widened. He put his hand on her shoulder. "Did you say this Hurlburt came back with the Indians?"

Seriously she nodded. "I saw him. He was in back of them, but I saw him. He was the one who shot his gun at Mister Ballard."

"You say he came back?" London asked. "You mean he went away from the wagons before the attack?"

She looked at him. "Oh, yes! He went away when we stopped by the big pool. Mister Ballard

164

and Daddy caught him taking things again. They put ropes on him, on his hands and his feet. But when morning came, I went to see, and he was gone away. Daddy said he had left the wagons, and he hoped nothing would happen to him."

Hurlburt. He had gone away and then had come back with the Indians. A renegade, then. What had they said of him in Independence? He had been over the trail several times. Maybe he was working with the Indians.

Betty Jane went to sleep on the grass he had pulled for her to lie on, and Jim London made a careful reconnaissance of the area, and then returned and lay down himself. After a long time he dozed, dreaming of Jane. He awakened feeling discouraged, with the last of their food gone. He had not tried the rifle, although twice they had seen antelope. There was too much chance of being heard by Indians.

Betty Jane was noticeably thinner, and her face looked wan as she slept. Suddenly he heard a sound and looked up, almost too late. Not a dozen feet away a Comanche looked over the reeds and aimed a rifle at him! Hurling himself to one side, he jerked out one of the Navy pistols. The Comanche's rifle bellowed, and then Jim fired. The Indian threw up his rifle and fell over backward and lay still.

Carefully London looked around. The rim of the hills was unbroken, and there was no other

Indian in sight. The Indian's spotted pony cropped grass not far away. Gun in hand, London walked to the Indian. The bullet from the pistol had struck him under the chin and, tearing out the back, had broken the man's neck. A scarcely dry scalp was affixed to his rawhide belt, and the rifle he carried was new.

He walked toward the horse. The animal shied back. "Take it easy, boy," London said softly. "You're all right." Surprisingly the horse perked up both ears and stared at him.

"Understand English, do you?" he said softly. "Well, maybe you're a white man's horse. We'll see."

He caught the reins and held out a hand to the horse. It hesitated, and then snuffed of his fingers. He moved up the reins to it and touched a palm to the animal's back. The bridle was a white man's, too. There was no saddle, however, only a blanket.

Betty Jane was crying softly when he reached her, obviously frightened by the guns. He picked her up, and then the rifle, and started back toward the horse. "Don't cry, honey. We've got a horse now."

She slept in his arms that night, and he did not stop riding. He rode all through the night until the little horse began to stumble, and then he dismounted and led the horse while Betty Jane rode. Just before daylight they rested.

Two days later, tired, unshaven, and bedraggled, Jim London rode down the dusty street of Cimarron toward the Maxwell House. It was bright in the afternoon sunlight, and the sun glistened on the flanks and shoulders of the saddled horses at the hitch rail. Drawing up before the house, London slid from the saddle. Maxwell was standing on the wide porch, staring down at him, and beside him was Tom Boggs, who London remembered from Missouri as the grandson of Daniel Boone.

"You look plumb tuckered, stranger, and that looks like an Injun rig on the horse. Or part of it."

"It is. The Indian's dead." He looked at Maxwell. "Is there a woman around here? This kid's nigh dead for rest and comfort."

"Sure!" Maxwell exclaimed heartily. "Lots of women around. My wife's inside." He took the sleeping child and called to his wife. As he did so, the child's eyes opened and stared, and then the corners of her mouth drew down and she screamed. All three men turned to where she looked. Hurlburt was standing there, gaping at the child as if the earth had opened before him.

"What is it?" Maxwell looked perplexed. "What's the matter?"

"That's the man who killed Mister Ballard! I saw him!"

Hurlburt's face paled. "*Aw,* the kid's mistook

me for somebody else," he scoffed. "I never seen her before." He turned to Jim London. "Where'd you find that youngster?" he demanded. "Who are you?"

Jim London did not immediately reply. He was facing Hurlburt and suddenly all his anger and irritation at the trail, the Indians, the awful butchery around the wagons returned to him and boiled down to this man. A child without parents because of this man.

"I picked that child up on the ground near a burned-out, Indian-raided wagon train," he said. "The same train you left Missouri with."

Hurlburt's face darkened with angry blood.

"You lie," he declared viciously. "You lie!"

Jim did not draw. He stared at Hurlburt, his eyes unwavering. "How'd you get here, then? You were in Independence when I left there. No wagons passed us. You had to be with that Ballard train."

"I ain't been in Independence for two years," Hurlburt blustered. "You're crazy and so's that blasted kid."

"Seems kind of funny," Maxwell suggested, his eyes cold. "You sold two rifles after you got here, and you had gold money. There's a train due in, the boys tell me. Maybe we better hold you until we ask them if you were in Independence."

"Like hell!" Hurlburt said furiously. "I ain't no renegade, and nobody holds me in no jail!"

Jim London took an easy step forward. "These guns I'm wearing, Hurlburt, belonged to Jones. I reckon he'd be glad to see this done. You led those Indians against those wagons. They found out you were a thief and faced you with it. I got it from Betty Jane, and the kid wouldn't lie about a thing like that. She told me all about it before we got here. So you don't get to go to jail. You don't get to wait. You get a chance to reach for a gun, and that's all."

Hurlburt's face was ugly. Desperately he glanced right and left. A crowd had gathered, but nobody spoke for him. He was up against it and he knew it. Suddenly he grabbed for his guns. Jim London's Prescott Navies leaped from their holsters, and the right one barked, a hard sharp report. Hurlburt backed up two steps, and then fell face down, a blue hole over his eye.

"Good work," Boggs said grimly. "I've had my doubts about that *hombre*. He never does nothing, but he always has money."

"Staying around?" Maxwell asked, looking at London.

"No," Jim said quietly. "My wife's waiting for me. I ain't seen her since 'Sixty-One."

"Since 'Sixty-One?" Boggs was incredulous. "You heard from her?"

"She didn't know where I was. Anyway, she never learned to write none." He flushed slightly. "I can't, neither. Only my name."

Lucian Maxwell looked away, clearing his throat. Then he said very carefully: "Better not rush any, son. That's a long time. It'll soon be five years."

"She'll be waiting." He looked at them, one to the other. "It was the war. They took me in the Army, and I fought all through."

"What about the kid?" Boggs asked.

"Come morning she'll be ready, I reckon. I'll take her with me. She'll need a home, and I sort of owe her something for this here rifle and the guns. Also"—he looked at them calmly—"I got nine hundred dollars in gold and bills here in my pocket. It's hers. I found it in her daddy's duffel." He cleared his throat. "I reckon that'll buy her a piece of any place we got and give her a home with us for life. We wanted a little girl, and while my wife . . . she was expecting . . . I don't know if anything come of it."

Both men were silent, and finally Maxwell said: "See here, London, your wife may be dead. She may have married again. Anyway, she couldn't have stayed on that ranch alone. Man, you'd better leave the child here with us. Take the money. You earned it, packing her here, but let her stay until you find out."

London shook his head patiently. "You don't understand," he said, "that's my Jane who's waiting. She told me she'd wait for me, and she don't say things light. Not her."

"Where is she?" Maxwell asked curiously.

"We got us a place up on North Fork. Good grass, water, and timber. The wife likes trees. I built us a cabin there, and a lean-to. We aimed to put about forty acres to wheat and maybe set us up a mill." He looked up at them, smiling a little. "Pa was a miller, and he always said to me that folks need bread wherever they are. 'Make a good loaf,' he said, 'and you'll always have a good living.' He had him a mill up Oregon way."

"North Fork?" Boggs and Maxwell exchanged glances. "Man, that country was run over by Injuns two years ago. Some folks went back up there, but one o' them is Bill Ketchum. He's got a bunch running with him no bettern'n he is. Hoss thieves, folks reckon. Most anything to get the 'coon."

When he rounded the bend below the creek and saw the old bridge ahead of him, his mouth got dry and his heart began to pound. He walked his horse, with the child sitting before him and the carbine in its scabbard. At the creek he drew up for just a moment, looking down at the bridge. He had built it with his own hands. Then his eyes saw the hand rail on the right. It was cut from a young poplar. He had used cedar. Somebody had worked on that bridge recently.

The cabin he had built topped a low rise in a clearing backed by a rocky overhang. He rode through the pines, trying to quiet himself. It might be like they said. Maybe she had sold out and gone away, or just gone. Maybe she had married somebody else, or maybe the Indians. . . .

The voice he heard was coarse and amused. "Come off it!" the voice said. "From here on you're my woman. I ain't takin' no more of this guff!"

Jim London did not stop his horse when it entered the clearing. He let it walk right along, but he lifted the child from in front of him and said: "Betty Jane, that lady over yonder is your new ma. You run to her now, an' tell her your name is Jane. Hear me?"

He lowered the child to the ground and she scampered at once toward the slender woman with the wide gray eyes who stood on the step staring at the rider.

Bill Ketchum turned abruptly to see what her expression meant. The lean, raw-boned man on the horse had a narrow sun-browned face and a battered hat pulled low. The rider shoved it back now and rested his right hand on his thigh. Ketchum stared at him. Something in that steel-trap jaw and those hard eyes sent a chill through him.

"I take it," London said gravely, "that you are Bill Ketchum. I heard what you said just now. I also heard down the line that you were a horse thief, maybe worse. You get off this place now, and don't ever come back. You do and I'll shoot you on sight. Now get!"

"You talk mighty big." Ketchum stared at him, anger rising within him. Should he try this fellow? Who did he think he was, anyway?

"I'm big as I talk," London said flatly. "I done killed a man yesterday down to Maxwell's. *Hombre* name of Hurlburt. That's all I figure to kill this week unless you want to make it two. Start moving now."

Ketchum hesitated, then viciously reined his horse around and started down the trail. As he neared the edge of the woods, rage suddenly possessed him. He grabbed for his rifle and instantly a shot rang out and a heavy slug gouged the butt of his rifle and glanced off.

Beyond him the words were plain. "I put that one right where I wanted it. This here's a seven-shot repeater, so if you want one through your heart, just try it again."

London waited until the man had disappeared in the trees, and a minute more. Only then did he turn to his wife. She was down on the step with her arm around Betty Jane, who was sobbing happily against her breast.

"Jim," she whispered. "Oh, Jim."

He got down heavily. He started toward her, and then stopped. Around the corner came a boy of four or five, a husky youngster with a stick in his hand and his eyes blazing. When he saw Jim, he stopped abruptly. This stranger looked just like the old picture on his mother's table. Only he had on a coat in the picture, a store-bought coat.

"Jim." Jane was on her feet now, color coming back into her face. "This is Little Jim. This is your son."

Jim London swallowed and his throat suddenly filled. He looked at his wife and started toward her. He felt awkward, clumsy. He took her by the elbows. "Been a long time, honey," he said hoarsely, "a mighty long time."

She drew back a little nervously. "Let's . . . I've coffee on. We'll. . . ." She turned and hurried toward the door, and he followed.

It would take some time. A little time for both of them to get over feeling strange, and maybe more time for her. She was a woman, and women needed time to get used to things.

He turned his head and almost automatically his eyes went to that south forty. The field was green with a young crop. Wheat! He smiled.

She had filled his cup; he dropped into a seat, and she sat down opposite him. Little Jim looked awkwardly at Betty Jane, and she stared at him with round, curious eyes.

"There's a big frog down by the bridge," Little Jim said suddenly. "I bet I can make him hop."

They ran outside into the sunlight, and across the table Jim London took his wife's hand. It was good to be home. Mighty good.

FORK
YOUR OWN
BRONCS

Mac Marcy turned in the saddle and, resting his left hand on the cantle, glanced back up the arroyo. His lean, brown face was troubled. There were cattle here, all right, but too few.

At this time of day, late afternoon and very hot, there should have been a steady drift of cattle toward the water hole.

Ahead of him he heard a steer bawl and then another. Now what? Above the bawling of the cattle he heard another sound, a sound that turned his face gray with worry. It was the sound of hammers.

He needed nothing more to tell him what was happening. Jingle Bob Kenyon was fencing the water hole!

As he rounded the bend in the wash, the sound of hammers ceased for an instant, but only for an instant. Then they continued with their work.

Two strands of barbed wire had already been stretched tight and hard across the mouth of the wash. Several cowhands were stretching the third wire of what was obviously to be a four-wire fence.

Already Marcy's cattle were bunching near the fence, bawling for water.

As he rode nearer, two men dropped their hammers and lounged up to the fence. Marcy's eyes narrowed and his gaze shifted to the big man on the roan horse. Jingle Bob Kenyon was watching him with grim humor.

Marcy avoided the eyes of the two other men by the fence, Vin Ricker and John Soley, who could mean only one thing for him—trouble, bad trouble. Vin Ricker was a gun hand and a killer. John Soley was anything Vin told him to be.

"This is a rotten trick, Kenyon," Marcy declared angrily. "In this heat my herd will be wiped out."

Kenyon's eyes were unrelenting. "That's just tough," he stated flatly. "I warned you when you fust come in here to git out while the gittin' was good. You stayed on. You asked for it. Now you take it or git out."

Temper flaring within him like a burst of flame, Marcy glared. But deliberately he throttled his fury. He would have no chance here. Ricker and Soley were too much for him, let alone the other hands and Kenyon himself.

"If you don't like it," Ricker sneered, "why don't you stop us? I hear tell you're a plumb salty *hombre*."

"You'd like me to give you a chance to kill me, wouldn't you?" Marcy asked harshly. "Someday

I'll get you without your guns, Ricker, and I'll tear down your meat house."

Ricker laughed. "I don't want to dirty my hands on you, or I'd come over an' make you eat those words. If you ever catch me without these guns, you'll wish to old Harry I still had 'em."

Marcy turned his eyes away from the gunman and looked at Kenyon.

"Kenyon, I didn't think this of you. Without water, my cows won't last three days, and you know it. You'll bust me flat."

Kenyon was unrelenting. "This is a man's country, Marcy," he said dryly. "You fork your own bronc's an' you git your own water. Don't come whinin' to me. You moved in on me, an', if you git along, it'll be on your own."

Kenyon turned his horse and rode away. For an instant Marcy stared after him, seething with rage. Then, abruptly, he wheeled his grayish-black horse—a moros—and started back up the arroyo. Even as he turned, he became aware that only six lean steers faced the barbed wire.

He had ridden but a few yards beyond the bend when that thought struck him like a blow. Six head of all the hundreds he had herded in here. By rights they should all be at the water hole or heading that way. Puzzled, he started back up the trail.

By rights, there should be a big herd here. Where could the cattle be? As he rode back toward his claim shack, he stared about him. No cattle were in sight. His range was stripped.

Rustlers? He scowled. But there had been no rustling activity of which he had heard. Ricker and Soley were certainly the type to rustle cattle, but Marcy knew Kenyon had been keeping them busy on the home range.

He rode back toward the shack, his heart heavy.

He had saved for seven years, riding cattle trails to Dodge, Abilene, and Ellsworth to get the money to buy his herd. It was his big chance to have a spread of his own, a chance for some independence and a home.

A home. He stared bitterly at the looming rimrock behind his outfit. A home meant a wife, and there was only one girl in the world for him. There would never be another who could make him feel as Sally Kenyon did. But she would have to be old Jingle Bob's daughter.

Not that she had ever noticed him. But in those first months before the fight with Jingle Bob became dog-eat-dog, Marcy had seen her around, watched her, been in love with her from a distance. He had always hoped that when his place had proved up and he was settled, he might know her better. He might even ask her to marry him.

It had been a foolish dream. Yet day by day it became even more absurd. He was not only in a fight with her father, but he was closer than ever to being broke.

Grimly, his mind fraught with worry, he cooked his meager supper, crouching before the fireplace. Again and again the thought kept recurring—where were his cattle? If they had been stolen, they would have to be taken down past the water hole and across Jingle Bob's range. There was no other route from Marcy's corner of range against the rim. For a horseman, yes. But not for cattle.

The sound of a walking horse startled him. He straightened, and then stepped away from the fire and put the bacon upon the plate, listening to the horse as it drew nearer. Then he put down his food, and, loosening his gun, he stepped to the door.

The sun had set long since, but it was not yet dark. He watched a gray horse coming down from the trees leading up to the rim. Suddenly he gulped in surprise.

It was Sally Kenyon! He stepped outside and walked into the open. The girl saw him and waved a casual hand, and then reined in.

"Have you a drink of water?" she asked, smiling. "It's hot, riding."

"Sure," he said, trying to smile. "Coffee, if you want. I was just fixing to eat a mite. Want to join me? Of course," he said sheepishly, "I ain't no hand with grub."

"I might take some coffee."

Sally swung down, drawing off her gauntlets.

She had always seemed a tall girl, but on the ground she came just to his shoulder. Her hair was honey-colored, her eyes gray.

He caught the quick glance of her eyes as she looked around. He saw them hesitate with surprise at the spectacle of flowers blooming near the door. She looked up, and their eyes met.

"Ain't much time to work around," he confessed. "I've sort of been trying to make it look like a home."

"Did you plant the flowers?" she asked curiously.

"Yes, ma'am. My mother was always a great hand for flowers. I like 'em, too, so when I built this cabin, I set some out. The wildflowers, I transplanted."

He poured coffee into a cup and handed it to her. She sipped the hot liquid and looked at him.

"I've been hearing about you," she said.

"From Jingle Bob?"

She nodded. "And some others. Vin Ricker, for one. He hates you."

"Who else?"

"Chen Lee."

"Lee?" Marcy shook his head. "I don't place him."

"He's Chinese, our cook. He seems to know a great deal about you. He thinks you're a fine man. A great fighter, too. He's always talking about some Mullen gang you had trouble with."

"Mullen gang?" He stared. "Why, that was in. . . ." He caught himself. "No, ma'am, I reckon he's mistook. I don't know any Chinese and there ain't no Mullen gang around I know of."

That, he reflected, was no falsehood. The Mullen gang had all fitted very neatly into the boothill he had prepared for them back in Bentown. They definitely weren't around.

"Going to stay here?" she asked, looking at him over her coffee cup, her gray eyes level.

His eyes flashed. "I was fixing to, but I reckon your old man has stopped me by fencing that water hole. He's a hard man, your father."

"It's a hard country." She did not smile. "He's got ideas about it. He drove the Mescaleros out. He wiped out the rustlers. He took this range. He doesn't like the idea of any soft-going, second-run cowhand coming in and taking over."

His head jerked up.

"Soft-going?" he flared. "Second-run? Why, that old billy goat."

Sally turned toward her horse. "Don't tell me. Tell him. If you've nerve enough."

He got up and took the bridle of her horse. His eyes were hard.

"Ma'am," he said, striving to make his voice gentle, "I think you're a mighty fine person, and sure enough pretty, but that father of yours is a rough-riding old buzzard. If it wasn't for that Ricker *hombre*. . . ."

"Afraid?" she taunted, looking down at him.

"No, ma'am," he said quietly. "Only I ain't a killing man. I was raised a Quaker. I don't aim to do no fighting."

"You're in a fighting man's country," she warned him. "And you are cutting in on a fighting man's range."

She turned her gray and started to ride away. Suddenly she reined in and looked back over her shoulder.

"By the way," she said, "there's water up on the rim."

Water up on the rim? What did she mean? He turned his head and stared up at the top of the great cliff, which loomed high overhead into the night. It was fully a mile away, but it seemed almost behind his house.

How could he get up to the rim? Sally had come from that direction. In the morning he would try. In the distance, carried by the still air of night, he heard a cow bawling. It was shut off from the water hole. His six head, starving for water.

Marcy walked out to the corral and threw a saddle on the moros. He swung into the saddle and rode at a canter toward the water hole.

They heard him coming, and he saw a movement in the shadows by the cottonwoods.

"Hold it!" a voice called. "What do you want?"

"Let that fence down and put them cows through!" Marcy yelled.

There was a harsh laugh. "Sorry, *amigo*. No can do. Only Kenyon cows drink here."

"All right," Marcy snapped. "They are Kenyon cows. I'm giving 'em to him. Let the fence down and let 'em drink. I ain't seeing no animal die just to please an old plug head. Let 'em through."

Then he heard Sally's voice. He saw her sitting her horse beside old Joe Linger, who was her bodyguard, teacher, and friend. An old man who had taught her to ride and to shoot and who had been a scout for the Army at some time in the past.

Sally was speaking, and he heard her say: "Let them through, Texas. If they are our cows, we don't want to have them die on us."

Marcy turned the moros and rode back toward his cabin, a sense of defeat heavy upon him. . . .

He rolled out of his blankets with the sun and, after a quick breakfast, saddled the grayish-black horse and started back toward the rim. He kept remembering Sally's words. There is water on the rim. Why had she told him that? What good would water do him if it was way up on the rim?

There must be a way up. By backtracking the girl, he could find it. He was worried about the cattle. The problem of their disappearance kept working into his thoughts. That was another reason for his ride, the major reason. If the cattle were still on his ranch, they were back in the breaks at the foot of the rim.

As he backtracked the girl's horse, he saw cow tracks, more and more of them. Obviously some of his cattle had drifted this way. It puzzled him, yet he had to admit that he knew little of this country.

Scarcely a year before he had come into this range, and, when he arrived, the grass in the lower reaches of the valley was good, and there were mesquite beans. The cattle grew fat. With hotter and dryer weather, they had shown more and more of a tendency to keep to shady hillsides and to the cañons.

The cow tracks scattered out and disappeared. He continued on the girl's trail. He was growing more and more puzzled, for he was in the shadow of the great cliff now, and any trail that mounted it must be frightfully steep. Sally, of course, had grown up in this country on horseback. With her always had been Joe Linger. Old Joe had been one of the first white men to settle in the rim country.

Marcy skirted a clump of piñon and emerged on a little sandy level at the foot of the cliff. This, at one distant time, had been a streambed, a steep stream that originated somewhere back up in the rimrock and flowed down here and deeper into his range.

Then he saw the trail. It was a narrow catwalk

of rock that clung to the cliff's edge in a way that made him swallow as he looked at it. The catwalk led up the face of the cliff and back into a deep gash in the face of the rim, a gash invisible from below.

The moros snorted a few times, but true to its mountain blood it took the trail on dainty feet. In an hour Marcy rode out on the rim itself. All was green here, green grass. The foliage on the trees was greener than below. There was every indication of water, but no sign of a cow. Not even a range-bred cow would go up such a trail as Marcy had just ridden.

Following the tracks of the gray, Marcy worked back through the cedar and piñon until he began to hear a muffled roar. Then he rode through the trees and reined in at the edge of a pool that was some twenty feet across. Water flowed into it from a fair-size stream, bubbling over rocks and falling into the pool. There were a number of springs here, and undoubtedly the supply of water was limitless. But where did it go?

Dismounting, Marcy walked down to the edge of the water and knelt on a flat rock and leaned far out.

Brush hung far out over the water at the end of the pool, brush that grew on a rocky ledge no more than three feet above the surface of the water. But beneath that ledge was a black hole at least eight feet long. Water from the pool was pouring into that black hole.

Mac Marcy got up and walked around the pool to the ledge. The brush was very thick, and he had to force his way through. Clinging precariously to a clump of manzanita, he leaned out over the rim of the ledge and tried to peer into the hole. He could see nothing except a black slope of water and that the water fell steeply beyond that slope.

He leaned farther out, felt the manzanita give way slowly, and made a wild clutch at the neighboring brush. Then he plunged into the icy waters of the pool.

He felt himself going down, down, down! He struck out, trying to swim, but the current caught him and swept him into the gaping mouth of the wide black hole under the ledge.

Darkness closed over his head. He felt himself shooting downward. He struck something and felt it give beneath him, and then something hit him a powerful blow on the head. Blackness and icy water closed over him.

Chattering teeth awakened him. He was chilled to the bone and soaking wet. For a moment he lay on hard, smooth rock in darkness, head throbbing, trying to realize what had happened. His feet felt cold. He pulled them up and turned over to a sitting position in a large cave. Only then did he realize his feet had been lying in a pool of water.

Far above he could see a faint glimmer of light, a glimmer feebly reflecting from the black, glistening roar of a fall. He tilted his head back and stared upward through the gloom. That dim light, the hole through which he had come, was at least sixty feet above him!

In falling he had struck some obstruction in the narrow chimney of the water's course, some piece of driftwood or brush insecurely wedged across the hole. It had broken his descent and had saved him.

His matches would be useless. Feeling around the cave floor in the dark, he found some dry tinder that had been lying here for years. He still had his guns, since they had been tied in place with rawhide thongs. He drew one of them, extracted a cartridge, and went to work on it with his hunting knife.

When it was open, he placed it carefully on the rock beside him. Then he cut shavings and crushed dried bark in his hand. Atop this he placed the powder from the open cartridge.

Then he went to work to strike a spark from a rock with the steel back of his knife. There was not the slightest wind here. Despite that, he worked for the better part of an hour before a spark sprang into the powder.

There was a bright burst of flame and the

shavings crackled. He added fuel and then straightened up and stepped back to look around.

He stood on a wide ledge in the gloomy, closed cavern at the foot of the fall's first drop, down which he had fallen. The water struck the rock not ten feet away from him. Then it took another steep drop off to the left. He could see by the driftwood that had fallen clear that it was the usual thing for the rushing water to cast all water-borne objects onto this ledge.

The ledge had at one time been deeply gouged and worn by running water. Picking up a torch, Marcy turned and glanced away into the darkness. There lay the old dry channel, deeply worn and polished by former running water.

At some time in the past, this had been the route of the stream underground. In an earthquake or some breakthrough of the rock, the water had taken the new course.

Thoughtfully Marcy calculated his situation. He was fearful of his predicament. From the first moment of consciousness in that utter darkness, he had been so. There is no fear more universal than the fear of entombment alive, the fear of choking, strangling in utter darkness beyond the reach of help.

Mac Marcy was no fool. He was, he knew, beyond the reach of help. The moros was ground-hitched in a spot where there was plenty of grass and water. The grayish-black horse would stay right there.

No one, with the exception of Sally, ever went to the top of the rim. It was highly improbable that she would go again soon. In many cases, weeks would go by without anyone stopping by Marcy's lonely cabin. If he was going to get out of this hole, he would have to do it by his own efforts.

One glance up that fall showed him there was no chance of going back up the way he had come down. Working his way over to the next step downward of the fall, he held out his torch and peered below. All was utter blackness, with only the cold damp of falling water in the air.

Fear was mounting within him now, but he fought it back, forcing himself to be calm and to think carefully. The old dry channel remained a vague hope. But to all appearances it went deeper and deeper into the Stygian blackness of the earth. He put more fuel on his fire and started exploring again. Fortunately the wood he was burning was bone dry and made almost no smoke.

Torch in hand he started down the old dry channel. This had been a watercourse for many, many years. The rock was worn and polished. He had gone no more than sixty feet when the channel divided.

On the left was a black, forbidding hole,

scarcely waist high. Down that route most of the water seemed to have gone, as it was worn the deepest.

On the right was an opening almost like a doorway. Marcy stepped over to it and held his torch out. It also was a black hole. He had a sensation of awful depth. Stepping back, he picked up a rock. Leaning out, he dropped it into the hole on the right.

For a long time he listened. Then, somewhere far below, there was a splash. This hole was literally hundreds of feet deep. It would end far below the level of the land on which his cabin stood.

He drew back. Sweat stood out on his forehead, and, when he put his hand to it, his brow felt cold and clammy. He looked at the black waist-high hole on the left and felt fear rise within him as he had never felt it before. He drew back and wet his lips.

His torch was almost burned out. Turning with the last of its light, he retraced his steps to the ledge by the fall.

How long he had been below ground, he didn't know. He looked up, and there was still a feeble light from above. But it seemed to have grown less. Had night almost come?

Slowly he built a new torch. This was his last chance of escape. It was a chance he had already begun to give up. Of them all, that black hole on the left was least promising, but he must explore it.

He pulled his hat down a little tighter and started back to where the tunnel divided into two holes. His jaw was set grimly. He got down on his hands and knees and edged into the black hole on the left.

Once inside, he found it fell away steeply in a mass of loose boulders. Scrambling over them, he came to a straight, steep fall of at least ten feet. Glancing at the sheer drop, he knew one thing— once down there, he would never get back up.

Holding his torch high, he looked beyond. Nothing but darkness. Behind him there was no hope. He hesitated, and then got down on his hands and knees, lowered himself over the edge, and dropped ten feet.

This time he had to be right, for there was no going back. He walked down a slanting tunnel. It seemed to be growing darker. Glancing up at his torch, he saw it was burning out. In a matter of minutes he would be in total darkness.

He walked faster and faster. Then he broke into a stumbling run, fear rising within him. Something brought him up short, and for a moment he did not see what had caused him to halt in his blind rush. Then hope broke over him like a cold shower of rain.

There on the sand beneath his feet were tiny tracks. He bent over them. A pack rat or some other tiny creature. Getting up, he hurried on, and, seeing a faint glow ahead, he rushed around a bend. There before him was the feeble glow of the fading day. His torch guttered and went out.

He walked on to the cave mouth, trembling in every limb. Mac Marcy was standing in an old watercourse that came out from behind some boulders not two miles from his cabin. He stumbled home and fell into his bunk, almost too tired to undress.

Marcy awakened to a frantic pounding on his door. Staggering erect, he pulled on his boots, yelling out as he did so. Then he drew on his Levi's and shirt and opened the door, buttoning his shirt with one hand.

Sally, her face deathly pale, was standing outside. Beyond her gray mare stood Marcy's moros. At the sight of him the grayish-black horse lifted his head and pricked up his ears.

"Oh," Sally gasped. "I thought you were dead . . . drowned."

He stepped over beside her.

"No," he said, "I guess I'm still here. You're pretty scared, ma'am. What's there for you to be scared about?"

"Why," she burst out impatiently, "if you. . . ." She caught herself and stopped abruptly. "After all," she continued coolly, "no one wants to find a friend drowned."

"Ma'am," he said sincerely, "if you get that wrought up, I'll get myself almost drowned every day."

She stared at him and then smiled. "I think you're a fool," she said. She mounted and turned. "But a nice fool."

Marcy stared after her thoughtfully. Well now, maybe. . . .

He glanced down at his boots. Where they had lain in the pool, there was water stain on them. Also, there was a small green leaf clinging to the rough leather. He stooped and picked it off, wadded it up, and started to throw it away when he was struck by an idea. He unfolded the leaf and studied the veins. Suddenly his face broke into a grin.

"Boy," he said to the moros, "we got us a job to do, even if you do need a rest." He swung into the saddle and rode back toward the watercourse, still grinning.

It was mid-afternoon when he returned to the cabin and ate a leisurely lunch, still chuckling. Then he mounted again and started for the old water hole that had been fenced by Jingle Bob Kenyon.

When Marcy rounded the bend, he could see that something was wrong. A dozen men were gathered around the water hole. Nearby and astride her gray was Sally.

The men were in serious conference, and they

did not notice Marcy's approach. He rode up, leaning on the horn of the saddle, and watched them, smiling.

Suddenly Vin Ricker looked up. His face went hard. Mac Marcy swung down and strolled up to the fence, leaning casually on a post.

"What's up?"

"The water hole's gone dry!" Kenyon exploded. "Not a drop o' water in it."

Smothering a grin, Marcy rolled a smoke.

"Well," he said philosophically, "the Lord giveth and He taketh away. No doubt it's the curse of the Lord for your greed, Jingle Bob."

Kenyon glared at him suspiciously. "You know somethin' about this?" he demanded. "Man, in this hot weather my cattle will die by the hundreds. Somethin's got to be done."

"Seems to me," Marcy said dryly, "I have heard those words before."

Sally was looking at him over her father's head, her face grave and questioning. But she said nothing, gave no sign of approval or disapproval.

"This here's a man's country," Marcy said seriously. "You fork your own bronc's and you get your own water."

Kenyon flushed. "Marcy, if you know anythin' about this, for goodness sake spill it. My cows will die. Maybe I was too stiff about this, but there's somethin' mighty funny goin' on here. This water hole ain't failed in twenty years."

"Let me handle him," Ricker snarled. "I'm just achin' to git my hands on him."

"Don't ache too hard, or you'll git your wish," Marcy drawled, and he crawled through the fence. "All right, Kenyon, we'll talk business," Marcy said to the rancher. "You had me stuck yesterday with my tail in a crack. Now you got yours in one. I cut off your water to teach you a lesson. You're a blamed old highbinder, and it's high time you had some teeth pulled.

"Nobody but me knows how that water's cut off and where. If I don't change it, nobody can. So listen to what I'm saying. I'm going to have all the water I need after this on my own place, but this here hole stays open. No fences.

"This morning, when I went up to cut off your water, I saw some cow tracks. I'm missing a powerful lot of cows. I followed the tracks into a hidden draw and found three hundred of my cattle and about a hundred head of yours, all nicely corralled and ready to be herded across the border.

"While I was looking over the hide-out, I spied Ricker there. John Soley then came riding up with about thirty head of your cattle, and they run 'em in with the rest."

"You're a liar!" Ricker burst out, his face tense, and he dropped into a crouch, his fingers spread.

Marcy was unmoved. "No, I ain't bluffing. You try to prove where you were about nine this morning. And don't go trying to get me into a gunfight. I ain't a-going to draw, and you don't dare shoot me down in front of witnesses. But you take off those guns, and I'll. . . ."

Ricker's face was ugly. "You bet I'll take 'em off! I allus did want a crack at that purty face o' yours."

He stripped off his guns and swung them to Soley in one movement. Then he rushed.

A wicked right swing caught Marcy before he dropped his gun belt and got his hands up, and it knocked him reeling into the dirt.

Ricker charged, his face livid, trying to kick Marcy with his boots, but Marcy rolled over and got on his feet. He lunged and swung a right that clipped Ricker on the temple. Then Marcy stabbed the rustler with a long left. They started to slug.

Neither had any knowledge of science. Both were raw and tough and hard-bitten. Toe to toe, bloody and bitter, they slugged it out. Ricker, confident and the larger of the two men, rushed in swinging. One of his swings cut Marcy's eye; another started blood gushing from Marcy's nose. Ricker set himself and threw a hard right for Marcy's chin, but the punch missed as Marcy swung one to the body that staggered Ricker.

They came in again, and Marcy's big fist pulped the rustler's lips, smashing him back on his heels. Then Marcy followed it in, swinging with both hands. His breath came in great gasps, but his eyes were blazing. He charged in, following Ricker relentlessly.

Suddenly Marcy's right caught the gunman and knocked him to his knees. Marcy stepped back and let him get up, and then knocked him sliding on his face in the sand. Ricker tried to get up, but he fell back, bloody and beaten.

Swiftly, before the slow-thinking Soley realized what was happening, Marcy spun and grabbed one of his own guns and turned it on this rustler.

"Drop 'em," he snapped. "Unbuckle your belt and step back."

Jingle Bob Kenyon leaned on his saddle horn, chewing his pipe stem thoughtfully.

"What," he drawled, "would you have done if he drawed his gun?"

Marcy looked up, surprised. "Why, I'd have killed him, of course." He glanced over at Sally, and then looked back at Kenyon. "Before we get off the subject," he said, "we finish our deal. I'll turn your water back into this hole . . . I got it stopped up away back inside the mountain . . . but, as I said, the hole stays open to anybody. Also"—Marcy's face colored a little—"I'm marrying Sally."

"You're what?" Kenyon glared, and then jerked around to look at his daughter.

Sally's eyes were bright. "You heard him,

Father," she replied coolly. "I'm taking back with me those six steers he gave you so he can get them to water."

Marcy was looking at Kenyon when suddenly Marcy grinned.

"I reckon," he said, "you had your lesson. Sally and me have got a lot of talking to do."

Marcy swung aboard the moros, and he and Sally started off together.

Jingle Bob Kenyon stared after them, grim humor in his eyes.

"I wonder," he said, "what he would have done if Ricker had drawed?"

Old Joe Linger grinned and looked over at Kenyon from under his bushy brows. "Jest what he said. He'd've kilt him. That's Quaker John McMarcy, the *hombre* that wiped out the Mullen gang single-handed. He jest don't like to fight, that's all."

"It sure does beat all," Kenyon said thoughtfully. "The trouble a man has to go to git him a good son-in-law these days."

About the Editor

Jon Tuska is the author of numerous books about the American West as well as editor of several short story collections, *Billy the Kid: His Life and Legend* (Greenwood Press, 1994) and *The Western Story: A Chronological Treasury* (University of Nebraska Press, 1995) among them. Together with his wife Vicki Piekarski, Tuska co-founded Golden West Literary Agency that primarily represents authors of Western fiction and Western Americana. They edit and co-publish twenty-six titles a year in two prestigious series of new hardcover Western novels and story collections, the Five Star Westerns and the Circle ⓥ Westerns. They also co-edited the *Encyclopedia of Frontier and Western Fiction* (McGraw-Hill, 1983), *The Max Brand Companion* (Greenwood Press, 1996), *The Morrow Anthology of Great Western Short Stories* (Morrow, 1997), and *The First Five Star Western Corral* (Five Star Westerns, 2000). Tuska has also edited a series of short novel collections, *Stories of the Golden West*, of which there have been seven volumes.

Center Point Publishing
600 Brooks Road ● PO Box 1
Thorndike ME 04986-0001 USA

(207) 568-3717

US & Canada:
1 800 929-9108
www.centerpointlargeprint.com